RIDE A
TALL HORSE

Also by Lewis B. Patten

GUNS AT GRAY BUTTE
PROUDLY THEY DIE
GIANT ON HORSEBACK
THE ARROGANT GUNS
NO GOD IN SAGUARO
THE GALLOWS AT GRANEROS
BONES OF THE BUFFALO
DEATH OF A GUNFIGHTER
THE RED SABBATH
THE YOUNGERMAN GUNS
POSSE FROM POISON CREEK
A DEATH IN INDIAN WELLS
SHOWDOWN AT MESILLA
THE TIRED GUN
RED RUNS THE RIVER
THE TRIAL OF JUDAS WILEY
THE CHEYENNE POOL
THE ORDEAL OF JASON ORD
BOUNTY MAN
LYNCHING AT BROKEN BUTTE
DEATH WAITED AT RIALTO CREEK
THE ANGRY TOWN OF PAWNEE BLUFFS
THE KILLINGS AT COYOTE SPRINGS
AMBUSH AT SODA CREEK
MAN OUTGUNNED
HUNT THE MAN DOWN
VILLA'S RIFLES
CHEYENNE CAPTIVES
THE LAW IN COTTONWOOD
THE TRAIL OF THE APACHE KID

RIDE A TALL HORSE

LEWIS B. PATTEN

DOUBLEDAY & COMPANY, INC.
GARDEN CITY, NEW YORK
1980

All of the characters in this book are fictitious, and any resemblance to actual persons, living or dead, is purely coincidental.

ISBN: 0-385-15714-2
Library of Congress Catalog Card Number 79-7844

Printed in the United States of America
First Edition

RIDE A
TALL HORSE

CHAPTER 1

Deputy Marshal McCabe had asked me to watch the office in Alkali Flat for him while he went to Tucson even though I was only eighteen and didn't actually work in the marshal's office. He said I was steady and he figured he could count on me not to do anything foolish.

I'm Jason Cole. I've got most of my growth because I stand six feet tall and weigh close to two hundred pounds. From the time my folks were killed by Apaches when I was eleven I'd done hard work for my keep so none of the two hundred pounds was fat although I did stumble over my own feet sometimes. Marshal McCabe said that was because I'd grown so fast and that I'd get over it.

On this particular furnace-hot day in July, I was sitting in the marshal's office with my feet on the desk, fingering a deputy's badge that I'd pinned on my sweat-stained shirt just to see how it would look on me. I'd admired myself in the mirror over the washstand a couple of times after making sure nobody was coming down the street. Now I was sitting there thinking what it was going to be like when I got made a deputy. Mr. McCabe had said he'd recommend me when I was twenty-one.

It was about ten o'clock in the morning when I heard the shot. I jumped and put my feet on the floor so quick that Marshal McCabe's swivel chair nearly scooted out from under me.

I owned a gun, an old .36 caliber Navy Colt's, but I never wore it. It was hanging, with its holster and belt, from the coat tree near the door. I crossed the room running and snatched the gun from its holster. I yanked open the door and plunged outside. I was in such a hurry that I tripped and sprawled face down on the worn boardwalk.

I muttered a couple of cusswords as I scrambled to my feet. I was thinking that the sound of the gunshot had to have been muffled, not only by the walls of the jail but by other walls as well. It had to have been fired indoors.

I started running uptown, thinking that someone might have been cleaning a gun, and I was hoping nobody had seen me fall when I saw a man come running out of Satterfield's Mercantile, a partly filled gunnysack in one hand, a revolver in the other.

There was a horse standing at the rail in front of Satterfield's. I knew that if I was going to stop the man I was going to have to throw any doubts I might have to the winds and shoot. He was a stranger. I'd heard a shot and he was in enough of a hurry so you sure as hell had to conclude he was running away. Besides, he had a gun in his hand. Marshal McCabe would've said that was prima facie evidence of a crime.

I stopped, plunked my butt down on the boardwalk and rested both forearms on my knees to steady them. I held the gun in both hands, got a bead on the man as he settled into his saddle, and squeezed off my shot.

He jerked, plainly enough so I saw it even at this distance. Then he spurred his horse away toward the upper end of town, which was north. I'd gotten his attention, though. He turned in his saddle and emptied his gun at me.

The bullets hit the street, kicking up spurts of dust, but

none of them came closer than ten or fifteen feet. I emptied my own gun, hoping for a lucky hit on his horse but it didn't do any good. He was out of the old gun's range.

As soon as the sound of gunfire died away, people began to come out of buildings and houses along the street. I got up and ran for Devlin's Livery Stable at the lower end. Marshal McCabe was gone. The town didn't have any other law officer so whatever was done was going to have to be done by me. I might be nervous and scared but I wasn't going to let anybody know it.

George Devlin was standing in the street looking toward the crowd in front of Satterfield's. I said, "Get the best two horses you've got. Saddle one and put a packsaddle on the other one. Then bring them up to Satterfield's."

He didn't question what I told him to do, which surprised me a little because I was used to taking orders, not giving them. I headed for Satterfield's at a dead run. The deputy marshal's badge was still on my shirt. I stopped at the jail long enough to get my belt and holster. The Navy Colt's had been converted from percussion to cartridges, and the belt was filled. I reloaded, fingers trembling in spite of myself. Then I got a Spencer repeating rifle from the gun rack and filled my pockets with cartridges for it. I went back out and ran toward Satterfield's again.

The door was jammed with people. Inside, I could hear someone crying hysterically. I pushed my way through.

I was soaked with sweat from running. At ten in the morning in July it's usually about a hundred and ten in the shade in the town of Alkali Flat. It seemed dark inside the store by comparison with the bright sunlight outside. And cool.

Leon Satterfield lay on his back on the floor, his old double-barreled shotgun lying beside him. There was a spot of blood about as big as the palm of my hand on his shirt front below his graying beard. The weeping I'd heard was coming from his daughter, Sue Ann, as pretty a girl as I was ever likely to meet. I'd been trying to court her for nearly a year with no encouragement from her. I had finally concluded I wasn't the kind of man she was looking for. Maybe she wanted more of a storekeeper type like her daddy was.

I knelt beside her and put my hand on her father's chest. There was no movement, either of heartbeat or breathing. He was dead. Awkwardly I lifted Sue Ann to her feet. She resisted me, but I was a lot stronger than she was. I turned her away from her father's body and put her in the hands of two middle-aged women. I said, "He's gone, Sue Ann. He's gone."

The words brought a new burst of hysterical weeping from her. It wasn't as if she had a mother or any other family. Her mother had died bearing her and there wasn't anybody else. I said, "I'll get the man, Sue Ann. I promise you." That wasn't much comfort, I knew, but it was about all I could think of to say that might make her feel a little better.

The two women, one on each side, pulled her through the crowd and into the street. Everybody seemed to have forgotten that I was only eighteen years old and had no authority. Maybe the badge pinned to my shirt and the gun hanging around my waist made the difference.

The first thing I did was walk to the back of the store where the safe was. It was a big, black thing, as tall as I was, trimmed with gilt scrolls with an eagle painted on the front in gold. Both doors stood open and the floor in front was littered with papers and ledgers. There was also an empty cashbox.

Mr. Satterfield had acted as banker for the town because it was too small to have a bank. I supposed there had been quite a bit of cash in that black metal box and all of it hadn't belonged to Mr. Satterfield. Those who had money on deposit with him would be wanting it replaced. Recovering it was damned important to Sue Ann and to the town.

It looked to me like the robber had come in, threatened Mr. Satterfield with his gun and forced him to open the safe. He'd stuffed the money into a gunnysack and started to leave.

Mr. Satterfield, conscious that most of the money being stolen wasn't his, must have grabbed his old shotgun and tried to make the robber stop. Doing so had cost him his life and hadn't accomplished anything.

I returned to the front of the store. I said, "All right, will all of you please go outside? Doc's here and there's nothing any of you can do."

Doc was the town drunk but at ten in the morning he was usually fairly sober even if he did have a hangover. He wasn't a real doctor anyway but a veterinarian. In any case, he was all the town of Alkali Flat had.

I followed the last of the people out, leaving Doc behind with Mr. Satterfield. George Devlin came riding up the street, leading a horse with a packsaddle and panniers on him. He pulled up at the rail, dismounted and looped the saddle horse's reins around the rail. He tied the packhorse's halter rope.

I cleared my throat and said, "I need three or four men to go with me. Who'll volunteer?"

Not a hand was raised. Jack Horseley asked, "Are you crazy? You can't go out there without an escort of cavalry. There's an Apache uprising in case you hadn't heard. There must be a dozen bands of Apaches on the loose."

I said, "That robber went out there. He don't seem to be all that scared of the Apaches. And you folks have got as much at stake. All some of you had was in Mr. Satterfield's safe."

A man said, "Wait for Marshal McCabe, son. He'll take a posse out just as soon as he gets back."

I supposed that was true. The marshal was due back sometime tomorrow, but I knew it would probably be late, which might mean day after tomorrow before a posse could leave Alkali Flat.

It would be smarter of me to wait for Marshal McCabe. I didn't have any authority and I didn't have any responsibility and I probably wasn't equal to the job. But I could hear Sue Ann Satterfield sobbing across the street in the shade of a building and I also knew that a forty-eight-hour delay would make trailing the fugitive mighty difficult.

I'd about decided to give it up when Sue Ann raised her tear-filled eyes and looked at me. I said, "I'm going anyhow, but I got to have supplies. Will one of you come inside and write down what I take off the shelves? The marshal's office will pay for the stuff in case—" I stopped. I'd been about to say, "In case I don't come back."

Jack Horseley, who sometimes worked for Mr. Satterfield, said he'd write down the stuff. I got the panniers off the packsaddle and carried them inside. I filled them with the things I thought I'd need. I got two new canteens, took them out back and filled them at the pump. I put them into the panniers so they wouldn't be jolting up and down.

Horseley had his list. I carried the panniers out and

hung them from the packsaddle, buckling the flaps to keep them closed and lashing them down with a rope, so they wouldn't be jolting up and down.

I'd always thought there'd be a lot of excitement in starting out after a fugitive, maybe even a certain amount of glory or at least admiration from the people who watched you go. There wasn't any of that. Nobody seemed to want to look at me. A man grumbled, "Stupid. That's what it is. A damn kid going out after a gunman. In Apache country too. It's stupid, that's what it is. McCabe will eat you for breakfast when he finds out what you've done!"

Sue Ann was different. She pulled away from the two women and came across the dusty street to me. She looked up, her face streaked with tears. She was still sobbing a little as she said, "You're the bravest man in town, Jason Cole. I'll pray for you."

With a lot more confidence than I felt I said, "I'll get him. Don't you worry about that," and I turned my horse and headed north out of town wishing I'd at least got a kiss to send me on my way.

I'd been alone since the Apaches killed my folks and burned everything they had. You'd think I'd be used to feeling lonesome, but as I rode out of town I felt more alone than I ever had in my life before. And more scared.

I got to the top of the first shallow rise, stopped and looked back. There wasn't anybody on the street. They'd all hurried in out of the sun.

The land north of Alkali Flat is almost flat and stretches away for about fifteen miles to the first range of rocky, barren mountains. I'd heard it said that this was all a big lake once millions of years ago and I guess it's true because you can find all kinds of fossils in the sandstone if you look. Fish and ferns and such. In some places there's a coating of white alkali, which is what gave the town its name.

The trail wasn't hard to follow. In fact, I didn't even have to follow trail. I could see him, a speck in the distance.

He had galloped for about half a mile, maybe figuring he was going to be chased right away. Then he must have realized that his horse wouldn't travel far at that gait in this heat so he'd slowed him to a trot. A couple of miles farther on, he pulled his horse back to a walk.

I had a big old silver watch that Marshal McCabe had taken off a drifter that died in Alkali Flat without any papers on him to let us know who he was and whether or not he had any family. There'd also been ten dollars and some change, which was enough to bury him. The marshal said he couldn't think what to do with the watch except give it to me.

It had a stag in midleap on the hunting-case cover and some pine boughs embossed on the back. I dragged it out of my pocket now and looked at it. It was nearly eleven o'clock.

Anybody with any sense stopped traveling between eleven and two or three o'clock. Especially in the summertime. But I knew the fugitive wouldn't stop and if he didn't I couldn't either.

Marshal McCabe had been kind of like a father to me and he'd tried to teach me the things he figured I ought to know. He'd taught me to trail where there weren't any clear tracks. He'd learned that from the Apaches and while he said he wasn't anywhere near as good as they were, he could get by trailing almost anybody *but* an Indian. About a year before he'd told me I'd learned all he could teach me and the rest I'd have to learn from practice.

Along the way, he'd taught me something much more important than just following trail. He'd taught me to try outthinking whoever it was you were following. If you could guess what they intended to do before they did it, there wasn't as much chance of you losing them or getting taken by surprise.

I started thinking about the man ahead of me. He'd committed a murder—of a prominent citizen—and he'd taken a lot of money for a small town like Alkali Flat to lose. He must know Satterfield's had been the only safe in town and that most of the town's savings were probably on deposit there. He probably had known that Marshal McCabe was out of town. But he also knew that when McCabe returned there would be a posse on his trail. So far, he probably didn't even know about me unless he'd looked back and seen my dust.

This killer also knew that the desert and surrounding mountains were swarming with hostiles. They didn't like the reservation at San Carlos and had tried to get themselves moved to the mountains in the north. They'd been refused. Now any Apache buck who could get half a dozen others to follow him had left, taking women and children and all the horses they could steal. Among these were Geronimo and Natchez, as cold-blooded a pair of killers as ever lived.

The desert in July isn't a very hospitable place to try and stay alive. Water holes dry up and streams sink into the ground. All the small bands of Apaches would be looking for sustenance and for more horses because they would have exhausted or eaten their own. No lone traveler would stay alive if they discovered him. No ranch would remain unmolested for very long. The cavalry had patrols out, but they were too few and far between.

As plain as I could see the man I was following, I had to figure he saw me too. So now I tried to figure out what he was thinking and what his plans were for getting rid of me.

He'd be able to see that I had two horses. He'd know the second was a packhorse loaded with supplies. Besides getting rid of me, he'd want that packhorse, as well as the one I was riding if he could manage it.

So he'd lay an ambush as soon as we got into the mountains where it was possible.

I began to wonder if I hadn't bit off more than I could chew. Then I thought, "You're eighteen. If you're ever going to be a man, it's time to start." I told myself that but I wasn't really convinced. I was still an inexperienced kid and I was scared.

Maybe so. But I was going to have to ride tall for the next few days.

CHAPTER 2

Where the first barren slopes of the mountains rose from the flatland, there was a huge organ-pipe cactus plant. Ahead, I saw the killer spurring his horse, just disappearing over the crest of the first high ridge. He'd had to slow his mount and stop him frequently going up that slope or he'd never have made it to the top.

I stopped beside the huge cactus, which provided enough shade for both my horse and myself. I made a big thing out of loosening cinches and lifting the panniers off the packsaddle. Then I pushed back my hat and sat down. I figured the robber had stopped as soon as he was out of sight since his horse needed rest a hell of a lot more than my two did.

I laid down and pulled my hat over my eyes, but I had positioned myself so that I could watch the top of the ridge.

The killer appeared, leading his horse. Even if I couldn't see, I knew his horse was lathered. It was too far to tell for sure, but I thought I could see him trembling. The man stared hard at me, then lifted his glance and stared back toward Alkali Flat.

He paced back and forth, like he was puzzled. He'd probably counted on a posse being hot on his trail by now, not just a single man. It was reassuring to realize that he had no way of knowing how old I was. Or how inexperienced.

Suddenly he seemed to realize that he and his horse were in the sun while I and my horses were in the shade. He mounted and disappeared.

I laid there thinking. A fly buzzed around my ear and I batted at it a couple of times. Mr. McCabe had always told me a lawman's mind is his best weapon if he takes the time and trouble to use it. Right now I figured was a good time to start using mine.

I knew one thing the killer did not. No posse was coming today.

I also realized that there was little chance I'd lose the trail. It never rained this time of year. The wind that came up in the afternoon wasn't strong enough to obliterate a trail except in a few spots where it was exposed. So I wasn't going to lose my man unless the Apaches got him before I did.

I rested there until both my horses had dried off. Then I got up and tightened the cinches. I mounted and, leading the packhorse, rode out again. Only I didn't try climbing straight up the steep, rocky slope. Instead I turned right along the base of the ridge. There was a draw over this way about a quarter mile. It would bring me out a hundred yards from where I'd last seen the killer and with a lot less effort for my horses.

I tried to decide what the fugitive was most likely to do next. He probably wasn't much afraid of me because I was only one. What he *was* afraid of was the posse that he figured would be coming later on. He'd want to put as many miles between himself and Alkali Flat as he could. He'd like to slow down and save his horse so that he could travel all night, but I was making that impossible.

So, unless he had a fresh horse stashed away someplace up ahead, he'd have to try to get rid of me.

The bottom of the ravine was sandy and rose in rocky stairsteps toward the crest of the ridge. Centuries of cloudbursts had formed it, and nowadays during any one of these cloudbursts it emptied enough muddy water into the Gato Grande River, which ran through town, to cloud it for miles downstream.

I halted frequently. Sweat had soaked my shirt and the seat and legs of my pants. The horses were already soaked again.

About halfway up the draw I stopped. Plainly in the sandy bottom of it, I saw the tracks of several unshod ponies crossing from left to right.

I didn't have to dismount to see how fresh they were. Moreover, there were a few horse droppings where the trail climbed out of the gulch that were so fresh they were still shiny.

I froze. I didn't see how this little bunch of Apaches could have missed the fugitive unless maybe they'd crossed in front of him while he was watching me lolling in the shade of the organ-pipe.

Holding my saddle horse as still as I could, I listened intently. I heard no sound of hoof on rock, or sound of rock dislodged. Breathing a little easier, I continued up the draw.

What the hell was a band of renegade Apaches doing this close to Alkali Flat? I wondered. Just passing by? Or was there another reason that I hadn't figured out?

Anyhow, I hoped they kept on going. I had enough trouble what with Satterfield's killer probably laying an ambush for me.

Another thought struck me, one that scared me more.

The Apaches whose trail I'd crossed were close enough to hear any shots fired, either by the fugitive or by me. And the minute they heard shots they'd turn around and come hotfooting back to see if they couldn't mix in and maybe pick up some horses and some guns.

When I got to the crest of the ridge, I dismounted. I concealed my horses below the crest so they'd not be skylined, and then I bellied down on the ground and looked at the terrain into which the fugitive had gone.

The mountains were like all the mountains that rise out of the Sonora desert, whether it be on the northern side of the border or the south. They were steep and rocky and barren. The only thing that grew on them was cactus: saguaro, organ-pipe, barrel, cholla, and half a dozen other varieties. There was also mesquite, and an occasional ironwood tree, and the tall, graceful stalks of the ocotillo, which puts out leaves all along each stalk every time it rains.

But I wasn't looking at the cactus or thinking about it. What I was looking for was the easiest route through the mountains ahead. Or at least what would look like the easiest route to a stranger viewing it.

The easiest way sure as hell wasn't from crest to crest. You had to look for a drainage and follow that. And since all drainages led south to the Gato Grande River, what the fugitive would be looking for was a big one, a main drainage, that climbed away toward the north.

Having grown up here, I knew the country around Alkali Flat pretty well. For the rest of today the fugitive would take Big Dry Creek, which had a fairly broad, sandy bottom, because it would be easy on his horse. Come night, he'd pick himself another route where tracks weren't so easy to see.

From where I was, I could see the broad gash made in the mountains by Big Dry Creek. I scowled because I knew I had to take it too. Unless I wanted to kill my horses making them go up and down and up and down all the rest of the day. But I didn't like the idea too much because I knew that was where the Apaches would be traveling too.

Before moving, I took a few minutes to scan every bit of country I could see, remembering the Apache trail I'd crossed a few times earlier. They had been going west, and I couldn't think of anything that might have made them turn back. Maybe by the time the fugitive decided to hide behind a boulder and take a shot at me, they'd be too far away to hear.

Seeing nothing, I slid my horse down the steep hill. The packhorse pulled back on the halter rope so I took a couple of turns around my saddle horn with it and after that he came along willingly.

Big Dry Creek, when it was running summer rainwater, emptied into the Gato Grande about half a mile above the town, that is, west of town. I angled toward it, taking my time. A worn-out horse will make a man plumb helpless and I didn't intend to let myself get into that kind of shape.

I reached Big Dry Creek, sliding my horses the last few yards and raising a cloud of dust. I hadn't gone a quarter mile before I picked up the trail of the fugitive.

His horse was now traveling at a walk. I thought about it some and finally decided the smartest thing for me to do would be to stop and kill about an hour. It would serve three purposes. It would rest my horses. It would give the small band of Apaches time to get out of hearing in case the fugitive took a notion to ambush me. And lastly, if he *had* laid an ambush, the fugitive would get tired of waiting before an hour passed. He'd begin thinking about the posse he thought would be coming and decide that maybe I'd gone back after finding out which direction he had headed in when he left Alkali Flat.

I got a canteen out of one of the panniers, poured a little into the palm of one hand and moistened the mouth and nostrils of my saddle horse. I did the same with the pack animal. There was a large bag of oats in one of the panniers and I fed each horse a handful, more to make them feel better than for any actual sustenance they'd get out of it.

I found myself a place where a huge weathered boulder gave off enough shade for both horses and myself, provided we got up real close to it because the sun was almost directly overhead. The horses availed themselves of the shade without being urged and I laid down on the sand and stared up at the sky. I wasn't worried about being surprised. I kept an eye on my horses' heads, knowing they'd see or smell anyone approaching a long time before I did.

I looked at my watch. It was now a little after noon. I wasn't hungry or thirsty, so I didn't eat or drink. I might be in for a long hard chase and before it was over with I'd likely need every drop of water and every morsel of food I had.

I closed my eyes occasionally against the glare, but I didn't doze. The horses stood there contentedly, switching at flies with their tails. I waited for what I thought was an hour and then looked at my watch again. It was nearly one.

Close enough. I got up, tightened both saddle girths

and mounted my saddle horse. The packhorse kept slack in the lead rope now so I didn't have to dally it.

The tracks were easy to follow and even from the back of my horse I could see how different they were from the way they'd been when I stopped. All the sharp edges had sloughed away.

I began daydreaming—about the way Sue Ann would look at me when I came in leading the fugitive's horse. Maybe he'd be dead, laid belly down across the saddle. Or maybe he'd be alive, riding upright with his hands tied behind his back and a scowl on his face because he'd been caught by a kid half his age.

I snapped myself out of that daydream fast. If I went on daydreaming, it would be me that died, only nobody would take me in. The buzzards would pick me clean. The man up ahead was ruthless or he wouldn't have shot Mr. Satterfield. He was desperate because he was wanted for murder now instead of for simple robbery. If he was caught, hanging was all he could look forward to. So he'd go to any lengths to avoid being caught.

The afternoon wore slowly away. I held my horses to a slow walk, gradually losing ground on the man I was following. Once, about four o'clock, I found a place where he *had* stopped, concealed himself and his horse behind a huge, rounded boulder and waited. Several Bull Durham cigarette butts had been ground into the sand where he had stood. There was a pile of horse droppings where he'd tied his horse. But he was gone. I guess he'd figured he couldn't afford to wait any longer. That hour-long rest I'd taken when I first hit the sandy bed of Big Dry Creek had probably saved my life.

I picked up my pace now, kicking my horse into a trot. The fugitive had tried an ambush and he wasn't likely to try another one today. Besides, he probably intended to travel a good part of the night and would thus gain four or five additional hours on me. Unless I wanted to take the chance that he'd stay in the creek bed and I did not. That would be what he'd expect me to do so he was almost certain to leave the creek bed as soon as it got dark.

By the time it was too dark to see his trail, I figured I was still more than half an hour behind. I found a place to stop where there were a few scrubby willows that the horses could browse on. Again I moistened their mouths and nostrils with a small amount of water. I took a sparing drink myself. Then I got a can of beans out of one of the panniers, opened it and ate the contents with my knife. I took another small swallow of water and laid down to sleep. It would be light enough to trail around four in the morning. I didn't need anything to wake me. First light would do that. But I looped the packhorse's halter rope around one wrist, knowing if any Apaches tried sneaking up on the camp he'd waken me.

The horse did wake me once, but only because he was reaching for a branch that happened to be out of his reach. After that I slept until dawn began to gray the eastern sky.

I gave each horse a sparing drink out of my fry pan. I fed each about a pint of oats. I got a handful of unsalted crackers for myself, then saddled up, mounted and rode out. Just as I had guessed, the fugitive had left the creek bed as soon as it got dark. And I hadn't been more than an hour behind when he did.

The sky was without a cloud. Already the temperature in this ravine must have been ninety-five. But a breeze was stirring in the south, blowing along the bed of Big Dry Creek and evaporating the sweat that had already soaked my clothes. The trail was a little harder to follow, but not hard enough to slow me down.

I got to thinking about Marshal McCabe. He was probably just leaving Tucson now. The stage would get into Alkali Flat about three in the afternoon and it would take him the rest of the day to get a posse organized and equipped.

Mr. Satterfield's funeral would probably be held today, I thought. It was too hot to wait. It might even be all over before Marshal McCabe got back.

I thought about Sue Ann. She'd never paid any attention to me before, but I couldn't forget her words, "You're the bravest man in town." Was it possible that she'd liked me all along and had just been too shy to let me know?

That was a pretty heady thought. I got to imagining what it would be like to hold Sue Ann in my arms and I began to sweat even more than I had been before. Then I remembered something Marshal McCabe had told me once. "When you're after a man, that's all you can afford to think about. You let your thoughts get to wandering and the first thing you know you've got a bullet in your brisket."

I forced myself to stop thinking about Sue Ann. The trail went up and down and up and down, heading pretty much north all the time.

Finally the fugitive struck a drainage leading west. I found where he'd clawed out a hole in the sand. He'd filled it in again but there was enough damp sand just below the surface to let me know he'd found water for himself and his horse.

I took time to dig the hole out and I let my horses drink. Then I mounted and took the trail again, now about four hours behind.

CHAPTER 3

I considered four hours to be a comfortable distance to have between myself and the fugitive. It wasn't likely he would wait that long to ambush me. For the first time since leaving Alkali Flat, I felt fairly safe.

Except, of course, for the possibility that a wandering party of Apaches would spot either me or the fugitive.

All day I stayed with the trail. It did not continue straight north but turned toward the northwest, heading toward the eastern edge of the Superstitions north of Tucson. The fugitive obviously had a destination. I didn't know what it was yet, but I would.

About midmorning on the day following the robbery and the murder of Mr. Satterfield, I came over a small ridge and looked down into a valley containing a small ranch. I backed my horse until only my head was visible to anyone below. I studied the ranch warily.

There was a corral, built from the twisted trunks of mesquite. There was a windmill, and therefore a well. There was a small house, roofed with sod, and an outhouse fifty feet away. There was a small chicken house. Beyond the house, down the draw, part of a hayfield was visible along with a couple of small fenced stacks.

One horse drowsed in the corral. Fifteen or twenty white chickens scratched in the dirt nearby, throwing up small plumes of dust. A few clothes hung limply from a clothesline stretched between the house and the outhouse. There were no other signs of life.

The fugitive's trail led straight down toward the house, but there was no sign of his horse, and since the trail was still at least four hours old, I had to assume he had stopped only briefly and had then gone on.

The fact that the ranch house had remained unmolested by the Apaches while most of the others within a hundred miles of San Carlos were said to have been attacked and burned was puzzling. Furthermore, it appeared to have been here several years.

Still puzzled and wary, I touched my horse's sides with my heels and, leading the packhorse, descended the bare and rocky slope. I held both my horse's reins and the packhorse's lead rope in my left hand and kept my right hand close to the grips of my holstered gun.

Halfway to the bottom, I heard a noise from inside the house. I stopped, my revolver half drawn. No one appeared so I continued to the bottom hurriedly.

The door was ajar. I swung from my horse, and with my revolver in my hand, I stepped quickly inside, shoving the door wide open as I did.

It seemed dark inside, but not too dark to see a man standing over a woman lying on the floor. As I glanced quickly around the room, looking for the killer I was pursuing, the man stooped and yanked the woman up. He drew back an already bloody fist to strike her again.

The woman's face was so bruised and bloody that I couldn't even tell what she looked like. I thought, "Oh, God, I've got myself right into the middle of a family quarrel." But it was the worst family quarrel I'd ever seen.

The man's back was toward me and for an instant the

woman's glance caught mine, held it just a moment and then slid away.

I knew that in another instant the man's fist would strike her bloodied face again. Without even thinking, I said shrilly, "Stop it!"

The man turned his head. "Where the hell did you come from?" He was big, no taller than my six feet but a whole lot heavier. He didn't seem to expect an answer to his question because he said, "This is private, son. Just get the hell out of here!"

Well, I was looking for a killer and for a lot of money and I know they'd both been here. I sure as hell wasn't going to wait politely outside while this man finished beating hell out of his wife.

The woman's glance met mine once more, without pleading, without expectation of any kind. Maybe it was this that decided me. I said, "No sir. You've hit her enough. Let her go."

As soon as the words were out of my mouth I knew I'd made a mistake. The man might let her go now and turn to me, which was all right, but after I was gone she'd catch it just that much worse.

The man flung the woman away from him. She crashed against the table, still making no outcry, caught herself and leaned against it, stunned and dazed, both of her eyes swelled nearly shut. The man turned to me.

I knew I couldn't use my gun breaking up a domestic quarrel. The man seemed to know it too. His eyes had not missed the deputy's badge pinned to the pocket of my shirt.

I thrust the gun down into my belt after easing the hammer down. I didn't like what I'd blundered into but it was too late to get out of it. Besides, I was hunting a man and he'd been here and there were a lot of things I had to know.

The man came toward me, not the least bit uncertain. To him, I was just a kid, but I'd been in a few fistfights. Enough to know I had a chance to beat this man if I didn't make any mistakes. Besides, there was something in the man's eyes that told me this was one fight I'd damn well better win.

The thought that I couldn't afford to make any mistakes had hardly taken form in my mind when the big man rushed. He didn't cock his fists first and he gave no sign that was what he was going to do. He simply plunged forward. His forearm struck me in the throat with enough force to slam me backward and send me tumbling out through the open door.

My windpipe felt as though it had collapsed. I couldn't get a breath of air into my lungs and the man was coming after me, a triumphant look already on his hard-looking, unshaven face.

I felt like I was finished. I couldn't get a breath. I couldn't seem to move. In another instant that big man was going to begin stomping me with his heavy boots. But then the man made his own mistake. He glanced aside at my saddle horse and at the cartridge belt hanging from the saddle horn as well as the rifle stock protruding from the saddle boot. His glance went past the saddle horse to take in the well-packed pack animal.

I grabbed for the revolver in my belt, but it was no longer there. Feeling real panic now, I scrambled forward along the ground and with the full force of my body, struck the big man just below the knees. The man went down like an undercut pine and I scrambled past him to come choking and gasping to my feet several yards farther on.

My chest burned like a fire was inside of it. I tried to swallow and could not. I didn't know how long I was going to be able to stay away from this big man but I hoped it would be long enough to let my throat open up and let some air into my lungs.

The man came up as I did, and slowly and confidently approached me. He acted like he had the whole day, like he knew how this fight was going to end and was therefore in no hurry to end it.

My eyes caught movement in the doorway of the house and I saw the woman standing there. It surprised me that there was nothing in her eyes, neither fear, nor dread, nor even hate. She was simply watching as if she already knew what the outcome was going to be and knew what would happen to her when it *was* over with. I also saw my gun, lying in the dust about halfway to the door.

I gasped, and coughed, and suddenly my windpipe opened up and I felt the precious, life-giving air flood my lungs. Still weak and dizzy, I circled, trying to make it to the gun before the big man saw it too.

But he had already seen the gun. Closer to it than me, he dived for it, both hands closing over it and holding on. He started to roll so that he could bring the gun to bear.

I thought, "My God, I'm going to get killed for messing in a family fight!" But I couldn't quit. As he rolled, I plunged forward, leaving my feet in a dive when I was close enough.

I struck the big man in the belly with both knees, driving a monstrous gust of air from him. With both hands, I tried to wrest the gun from him, at the same time trying to keep the muzzle from pointing itself at me.

Now it was this other man who couldn't get air into his lungs. I had driven every bit of it out of them when I landed on him. Yet his grip on the gun did not relax and, try as I would, I couldn't pry it loose. Furthermore, he was fighting still, and despite the fact that he couldn't get any air he was enormously strong. He raised both his legs, trying to get a scissors grip around my middle with them.

I evaded his legs, raised up and slid a knee under his right arm. With all my strength, I brought both my hands down then, hoping with the impact to break his grip on the gun.

I heard the bone crack in his right arm. He let out a cry that was half roar, half screech of pain. The gun fell from his hands.

I seized it, pulled away and made it to my feet. I hadn't intended to break his arm. Gun in hand, I stared at him, writhing with pain on the ground. Every movement he made increased the pain. When he finally realized that, he stopped writhing and, with his left hand, held the broken right arm against his belly.

Even now the damn fool didn't know he was beat. He made it to his feet and charged, half blind with pain, his right arm still held tight against his belly by his left hand.

I stepped easily out of his way and he staggered past, to collapse on the woodpile twenty feet away.

From the door, the woman's voice now came unemotionally, "If you let him get up, you'll either have to kill him or he'll kill you. He's got a piece of firewood in his good hand." Her voice, while unemotional, still managed to be pleasant, almost musical.

I wanted to look at her but there was no time. The man

was up and coming at me again, a thick piece of mesquite in his left hand, his right flopping uselessly at his side.

I stepped aside again and as the man charged blindly past, swinging the piece of mesquite firewood viciously at my head, I stuck out a foot. He sprawled out on the ground, losing his grip on the firewood.

I only had two choices. I could shoot him or I could knock him out. I stepped in close and kicked him in the head. The heel of my boot struck his forehead solidly and he went limp.

I'd won, but the fight had taken a lot out of me. My breath rasped noisily in and out. My chest heaved. My legs were trembling. It was the worst fight I'd ever been in because this time I had been fighting for my life.

I walked to my horse, took down the cartridge belt and after making sure an empty chamber was under the hammer thrust the gun into its holster. I belted it around my waist. Stooping, I picked up the stick of firewood and threw it the twenty feet to the woodpile. The woman said, "He's not going to stay unconscious very long."

I shrugged, sorry for what was in store for her, but remembering suddenly why I was here. I said, "I'm following a killer. He came through here. How long ago, and which way did he go when he left?"

As badly battered as was her face, I thought that something evasive touched it. Her eyes raised involuntarily and looked at something beyond the woodpile. Turning my head to follow the direction of her glance, I saw nothing but a stretch of ground where there were no rocks.

I looked back toward her but now she wouldn't look at me. She looked instead at her husband, lying unconscious on the ground. When she looked back at me she had made her decision. She said, "He is still here."

Alarm touched me. "Here? Where?"

"Over there." She pointed at the spot she had glanced at earlier.

I studied the spot more carefully, able now to make out a mound of freshly turned earth. And at last I understood—the big man's quarrelsomeness, his glance toward my horses, saddles and guns. I thought with sudden horror that this place was a human spider's web, in which travelers became entangled but from which few escaped.

I studied the woman more closely now, wondering if she could possibly be a part of it. Her hair was very dark, clean and shining but mussed from the beating her husband had given her. Her skin was light for an Indian but too dark for a white. She might be Mexican but I guessed she was Apache because only that would explain why these two were able to live unmolested in the middle of bands of marauding Apaches.

Still chilled with horror I asked, "How many has he killed?"

"Many. Count the graves."

I stared at the man on the ground unbelievingly. Until now I hadn't even realized that men like this existed. I asked, "What's his name?"

"Nathan Paddock."

"And yours?"

The faintest of smiles touched her battered lips. "My Apache name is too hard for white people to pronounce. At the agency at San Carlos I was called Luisa—Lu for short."

"Is that where you learned to speak English so well?"

She nodded.

I said, "I'll need some bandages to splint his arm."

"What are you going to do with him?"

"Take him in. He's a murderer."

She disappeared into the house to get bandages. I went to the woodpile and found a piece of mesquite thin and straight enough to splint Paddock's broken arm. I returned, got hold of Paddock's good arm and dragged him to the corral. I tied his feet together with a coil of rope that had been hanging from the corral gate, then passed the rope end around a post, brought it back out and tied Paddock's left wrist with it. I didn't want to have to fight him again and I knew that when he came to, broken arm or no, he'd fight.

Lu came out with a petticoat, which she began to tear into strips. When they were ready, and rolled individually, I bound the splint loosely to Paddock's arm. Then I sat down and braced my feet against Paddock's body. I took his right wrist in both hands and pulled. I felt the bone slip into place and said to Lu, "Now bind it up."

Paddock had regained consciousness for an instant when I first took hold of his arm. He lost it again when I pulled. He remained unconscious while Lu was doing the bandaging.

Finished, I got up and asked her where I could find a shovel. Leaving Paddock where he was, I walked to the fresh grave and began to dig.

Two feet down my shovel struck something soft. I carefully scraped earth away from the body, at the last using only my hands. I'd never seen Satterfield's killer up close enough to recognize his face. But I remembered what he'd been wearing. There was a blood spot on the front of his shirt that was still wet. There was another wound in his side. The blood that had soaked his shirt from this wound was dry and brown. I must have hit him there.

I lifted the body out, then climbed out myself. I carried the body to the shade of the house. Lu came out. She asked, "What did he do?"

"Killed a storekeeper during a robbery."

"I know where the money is."

I nodded, straightened and followed her into the house. The floor was of hard-packed earth, but there was a large, flat piece of sandstone in front of the fireplace that served as a hearth. I lifted it.

Inside the cavity underneath there was a large rusted and battered metal box filled with currency and coins, many of them gold. There were watches and pocket knives and various other items men carried in their pockets or saddlebags including a tintype of a woman in a small, oval-shaped gold frame. There were at least a dozen guns lying loose on a piece of canvas. I replaced the piece of sandstone over the opening.

I looked at Lu and asked, "Where are their horses? There's only one in the corral."

"Loose. Some of them are down in the hayfield, trying to get through the fences around the stacks."

"Can you catch a couple?"

She nodded.

While she went after the horses, limping slightly as she walked, I went to the corral, caught and saddled the horse inside. Paddock had regained consciousness. He said, "You'll never get me to jail, you young son-of-a-bitch. I'll bury you down there with the others."

I didn't answer him. I knew if I wasn't careful he'd do exactly what he said he would.

"You going to leave me tied up here?"

"Until we're ready to leave, I am."

All the time I was saddling the horse I could feel Paddock's stare. I thought about his wife. It was true that he beat her unmercifully, but that didn't mean no bond existed between them. I couldn't trust her not to cut her husband loose if she got the chance.

I tied the horse and walked back to the place I'd dug up the killer's body. I walked slowly and carefully, studying the ground. I counted five mounds similar to the one that had betrayed the location of the body I'd dug up earlier. All were older and therefore less noticeable and I knew there could be others I hadn't seen.

All these bodies would have to be dug up later and identified. For now I had all I could handle, getting Paddock, Lu and the killer's body back to Alkali Flat, without worrying about anything else.

With five horses, avoiding detection by the Indians was going to be difficult. Lu, being Apache, had kept Paddock safe from them simply because she was his wife. So Paddock wouldn't hesitate to try exposing us all to the Indians, knowing I would be the only one they'd kill.

I suddenly wished I'd waited for Marshal McCabe to get back from Tucson. Even so, I couldn't help feeling a little bit proud of myself. I'd caught up with the killer and recovered the money. In the bargain, I'd caught a mass murderer. All I had to do now was get safely back to Alkali Flat.

CHAPTER 4

I went back into the house, an adobe structure with a sod-covered roof. Lu had not returned with the horses and I wondered briefly if she would come back. It would be easy for her to just mount one of the horses and go back to her people on the reservation. Certainly she had plenty of justification for doing so.

I found a couple of gunnysacks. Into one I loaded all the money under the hearthstone and into the other I loaded all the guns, mainly to keep any Apaches from getting them. I figured I had enough provisions in the packsaddle panniers to last the three of us for the two or three days it was going to take to get back to Alkali Flat.

I carried the two sacks out and hung them on top of the panniers. Then I went back inside, looking for a piece of canvas big enough to sew the dead killer's body in. Three days in the desert heat would make it smell so bad none of us could stand being close to it. Sewing it into canvas now would help some. I could have reburied it, of course. But I was thinking about Sue Ann Satterfield, and wanting to look good in her eyes when I rode back into Alkali Flat.

Lu returned, leading two horses. She tied them outside and came into the house. I told her I wanted some canvas and she got a piece out from under the straw mattress on the bed. She found a big needle and some twine and I went out and began to sew the killer's body in the canvas, which was big enough to go around his body twice. Lu came out and took over, her hands a lot more skilled than mine. Watching her, I couldn't help noticing how straight and slim was her back, how slender her waist, how rounded her hips beneath her thin cotton dress and petticoat. There was no way I could tell what her face looked like, as badly beaten as it was, but if it was as beautiful as the rest of her, Paddock was lucky to have her and a fool for treating her so bad.

I went into a small lean-to at the rear of the house looking for a couple of saddles. The place was full of them, riding and packsaddles both. I picked two, along with saddle blankets and bridles, and carried them around in front. I saddled the two horses Lu had brought in.

By that time, she was finished sewing the killer in his canvas shroud. I hoisted him to my shoulder and laid him over one of the horses I had just put a saddle on. Knowing I would need it, Lu brought me a length of rope and I lashed the body down. I said, "If there's anything you want to take, get it now. We're leaving right away."

She went into the house and returned a few moments later with a small, cloth-wrapped bundle.

Paddock sure hadn't been generous with her, I thought, if that was all she had to show for living here with him. I asked suddenly, "How old are you and how long have you been married to him?"

"Seventeen. I was married to him when I was fifteen."

I crossed the yard to the corral, stooped and untied Paddock's feet, but I left the rope tied to his unhurt wrist. I stayed off the length of the rope away from him. I said, "Get on that horse."

"How, for Christ's sake?"

"You'll manage. Or walk."

He approached the horse. His face twisted with pain as he mounted, using only his left hand to pull himself up, but he had no real difficulty. I took a quick half hitch around one of his ankles and threw the end of the rope under the horse's belly. I went around and glanced up at him. I said, "You can try kicking me if you want, but I've got the end of this rope and if you do, I'll lash the horse's rump with it and dump you on the ground."

He snarled, "I've got a lot of things to remember when I get loose."

"If you ever do." I led the horse to where mine were. I tied the halter rope of my packhorse to the tail of Paddock's horse. Lu had already mounted. I got hold of the halter rope of the horse on which the body was lashed and handed it to her. We'd be strung out most of the time between here and Alkali Flat with not much chance to talk and something was bothering me. I looked at Lu and asked, "Why did you do it?"

"Do what?"

"Marry a man like him?"

"He gave my father three horses and a gun."

For some reason it made me feel better to be told she hadn't had a choice. But there were a couple more things I had to know. "Why was he beating you?"

"Because I tried to warn that man." She gestured with her head toward the man in the canvas shroud.

"Why didn't you run away from him?"

"Where would I go? I would not be welcome at San Carlos. My father accepted three horses and a gun for me. Besides, it is a husband's right to beat his woman if she does not please him."

"And what makes you think you didn't please him?"

"He would not have beaten me if I had."

I felt the lead rope to Paddock's horse begin to tighten in time to take a couple of turns with it around my saddle horn. I looked back. Paddock, who was on his own saddle horse, had tried to turn the animal aside with his knees, intending, as soon as the halter rope came loose, to make a run for it. I knew he'd try it again, and again, so I took down the lariat from my saddle, made a small loop, then moved back and placed it over Paddock's head. Moving ahead again, I clove-hitched it to my saddle horn so that it had only a little more slack in it than in the halter rope.

Lu had halted and was waiting. I said, "You go on ahead."

She obeyed. We rode down the valley and around the rocky point that had almost hidden the hayfield from the house. The hayfield was bigger than I had at first supposed, probably fifty or sixty acres in size. It was fenced, and inside the fence around the hayfield, each haystack was fenced separately so that the hayfield could be used as pasture after each cutting of hay.

Now that Paddock was secured by the lariat, I didn't have to worry about him much. The minute he tried getting it off I'd know it. But I stared ahead at Lu's back, wondering if I could trust her. She had stayed with Paddock two years despite the way he treated her. She admitted she had no place else to go. She had tried to warn the dead man before Paddock killed him, but that didn't mean she wouldn't try to help Paddock escape.

Furthermore, any Apaches we encountered would know both her and Paddock. They would not molest them; they would only try killing me.

I didn't figure I could go back the way I'd come. It would take too long and would be too hard on these horses. The only feed I had, for five horses, was the small amount of grain I'd brought to feed my two. Paddock hadn't had any grain and hay was too bulky to carry.

I figured Alkali Flat was southeasterly. If I headed straight south I'd strike the stage road between Alkali Flat and Tucson. Then maybe I could get some help.

I had hoped the valley in which Paddock had built his cabin would continue south, for a little ways at least, but it did not. A couple of miles south, it made a sharp bend toward the west. I asked Lu, "Does it keep going west or does it turn south again?"

"It keeps going west for about ten miles. Then it turns north into the mountains."

I headed south up into the mountains, stopping often to let the horses rest. It must have been close to a hundred and twenty in the shade if we could have found any shade. My whole body was soaked with sweat and the horses were lathered before we reached the first mountain crest. We'd have to travel mostly at night, I thought, because of both the heat and the danger from Indians.

The horses could go three days without food, provided they had water. But they'd be needing water before the sun went down tonight.

I wondered what Lu would do if we were attacked by Indians. She didn't have a gun, or at least I didn't think she had. And even if I provided her with one, I doubted if she'd use it against her own people. She could certainly have no love for whites. Not after her experiences with Paddock. Yet she had also said she could not return to the reservation at San Carlos.

Ahead of us stretched one barren ridge after another on

which nothing grew but a few barrel cactus, brown and partly dead. Traveling this kind of terrain was rougher and harder than traveling in a draw but it was a lot safer. Besides, for now, no drainages were available to us. None that led in the right direction at least.

In midafternoon Lu halted suddenly. I rode up beside her and she pointed to a trail, nearly paralleling ours and heading in the same direction. I studied it long enough to determine that there had been seven unshod ponies and that the trail was very, very fresh.

I turned my head and looked at Paddock. "One sound out of you and I'll blow your head off."

"That'll sure as hell bring 'em down on you."

"So it will. But you won't be alive to enjoy it."

I guess he decided I meant what I said because he made no attempt to alert the Indians. We sat our horses, keeping them as still as possible, which wasn't hard because they all were sweaty, thirsty and tired, and after a few minutes we sighted a file of seven half-naked Apaches climbing their ponies out of the ravine ahead.

I held my breath for fear one of them would look around. The slightest sound now and they'd turn and come after us. We had five horses they could use, guns and provisions. To Lu I whispered, "Watch them. If they turn and see us, let me know."

I withdrew my Navy Colt's from its holster and carefully eased back the hammer, knowing how even a small sound would carry across a ravine like the one ahead of us. I pointed it at Paddock. "You're a killer and you're going to hang. Just one little noise out of you and I'll save the hangman the trouble. Don't even clear your throat."

I kept my eye on Paddock, gun in my right hand, lariat that was looped around his neck in my left. The horses all stood with their heads hanging, too tired even to switch at flies with their tails or search for a clump of grass.

It seemed an eternity before Lu said softly, "They have gone over the ridge."

"Think they saw us?" With Apaches there was the possibility they'd let you think you had not been seen so that you'd ride blindly into an ambush they had laid.

"I do not think so. I think I would have known."

"What tribe did they belong to?"

"Chiricahua."

"Did you know any of them?"

She nodded. "The one in the lead was Natchez."

I whistled softly.

She smiled faintly. Her bruised and swollen mouth was looking better all the time. At least the swelling had partially gone down.

I waited, letting the horses rest. I wanted the Apaches to get several miles ahead of us before we went on again and besides the horses could use the rest.

I said, "Paddock is as good as dead. You'll be a widow. What will you do?"

Her expression was confused. "I don't know. I haven't thought about it."

"You'll have that ranch. That is if you were legally married."

"We were. The Indian agent insisted on it. But I cannot run a ranch alone. And besides, he would always be there. In spirit. In my mind."

I could understand that easily enough. I studied her face, which was suddenly filled with confusion. I was beginning to realize that when the swelling and scabs had gone, she would be a good-looking woman. Already I could tell that she did not have the flat features of the average Apache.

Down at the bottom of the ravine I could see a thick clump of tall mesquite. I said, "Ride down there. There's some shade." It might be even hotter in the ravine since the sun's rays collected there, but the shade would compensate.

Paddock said, "You trying to kill me with thirst? How about a drink?"

"Soon," I said. Lu rode carefully toward the bottom of the ravine.

At the bottom we dismounted. I went around loosening cinches. Lu kept her eyes on Paddock, who occasionally met her glance with a threatening scowl. I got one of the canteens and moistened all five horses' mouths and nostrils. Only then did I hand the canteen to Lu. She took a very sparing drink. I gave Paddock the canteen, holding it myself, and when I thought he'd had enough, I took it away. I took a sparing drink myself, knowing we might need this water more for the horses than for ourselves.

Lu sat down in the sparse bit of shade. Retaining my hold on the rope around Paddock's neck, I sat down a few feet away. I knew every movement of either body or face must cause her pain but she gave no indication of it.

Suddenly and without warning, Nathan Paddock uttered a piercing shout. I yanked savagely on the rope. The noose tightened, shutting off Paddock's air, instantly cutting off the shout. Keeping the noose tight, I got up and lunged to where Paddock sat. I'd promised him a bullet but I didn't want to take the chance. The Indians might possibly not have heard his shout. They'd surely hear a shot. Paddock tried to grab one of my ankles with his good hand. Out of patience, I yanked my revolver out and slammed it against his head. Paddock slumped.

I glanced at Lu. Her battered face was not mobile enough to show much expression but I thought I detected a glint of approval in her eyes. I said, "Tear some strips from your dress or petticoat. I'll have to gag him."

She raised her skirt, revealing shapely legs. Without embarrassment, she tore some strips from the thin petticoat beneath her dress and handed them to me.

I made a ball with about half of them and, prying open Paddock's mouth, stuffed them inside. Then I bound the others around his head to hold the gag in place.

I looked at Lu. "Do you think they heard?"

"I don't know. I don't think so. They must have been well down into the next ravine. And their horses would have been making some noise sliding on the rocks."

"You think we ought to stay here? Or get moving?" I didn't feel funny about asking her advice. She was, after all, Apache, and she knew a lot more about them than I ever would.

"I think we should stay until it is nearly dark. Then we can go on and find out which way they went. Afterward we can travel in the dark."

That sounded all right to me. I settled back and made myself comfortable so that I could see one hillside, the one opposite the hillside Luisa faced.

I was beginning to trust her, at least trust her not to give us away. But if it came to a fight, I didn't know what to expect of her. Would she fight her own people, taking sides with me, whom she scarcely knew, and a husband who had never done anything but abuse her?

It didn't seem reasonable. But alone I couldn't fight even that small group of seven we'd seen ahead of us.

Once more I wished I'd waited for Deputy Marshal McCabe to get back from Tucson and get a posse up. But I hadn't and now I was going to find out if I was as grown-up as I'd thought I was. I wasn't near as sure as I had been sitting there in the deputy marshal's chair back in Alkali Flat admiring the badge on my chest.

CHAPTER 5

The sun was well down in the western sky. In another half hour it would sink below the ridgetop west of us.

For a little while I sat still, studying the ridges in all directions, but mostly concentrating on the one ahead. Nothing moved. Paddock came to, struggled into a more comfortable position and began making muffled sounds behind the gag. Once he raised his good hand to try and yank it out. I said softly, "Don't, unless you want another knot on your head."

If looks could have killed, I'd have died right then.

There was something I figured I ought to find out right quick so I said to Lu, "You know those Indians ahead of us. What will you do if they attack us?"

Her mouth made the faintest of smiles despite its swollen condition. "Do you mean whose side will I take?"

"That was what I meant."

She said, "I am no longer a Chiricahua. I can't go back to them. I would do nothing for him"—she gestured with her hand toward Paddock—"but you saved me from him. He might have killed me if you had not come along." She paused a moment. "I can use a gun. If you will give me one, I will help you if they attack."

I got up and went to the gunnysack that contained all the guns I had found under Paddock's hearthstone. I found a .36 caliber Colt's that, like mine, had been converted to use cartridges. I loaded it from my cartridge belt and handed it to her.

Now I scanned the hilltops again. The sun had dropped out of sight, throwing the whole ravine into shadow.

I saw nothing so I got up, took an oat sack out of one of the panniers, and fed a double handful to each of the horses. After that I dampened their nostrils and mouths again.

It was dusk now, growing darker all the time. The rays of the sun no longer touched even the ridgetops to the east. I looked at Lu and she nodded. I put the lariat around Paddock's neck again and secured it to my saddle horn. I replaced the panniers and gunnysacks on the packsaddle. Lu mounted, holding the lead rope of the horse on which the dead man's body had been lashed. I nodded at her and she led out. I figured if I couldn't trust her, I was dead. And if I could—well, she was an Apache, possessing all an Apache's stealth and cunning as well as their uncanny ability to see in the dark, and to hear the slightest alien sound.

We climbed the ridge lying to the south, almost in the trail left by the seven Apaches. Lu halted at the top and both of us used what little light was left to carefully scan every hillside for signs of them. I knew she had seen nothing when she touched her horse's sides with her heels and he moved on down the slope.

By the time we reached the crest of the next ridge, it was completely dark. Occasionally I glanced back at Paddock. Even in the darkness I could see the white of the cloth strips binding the gag in his mouth. So far he had not made another attempt to get it out.

We climbed and descended seven rocky ridges before we finally struck a drainage that headed south. Its bottom was sandy, if less than a couple of dozen feet wide. Lu still had the lead, trailing the horse with the body on it. I came behind, and Paddock was behind me, with the packhorse's halter rope tied to the tail of his horse.

We had gone no more than a quarter mile when Lu suddenly stopped. I had sense enough not to call out to her. Instead I ranged my horse up beside hers. Her voice was the barest whisper. "I heard something."

She was off her horse before she had finished speaking and I hit the ground almost simultaneously. About fifty feet ahead of us, half a dozen rifles roared. I heard the distinctive smack of bullets hitting two of the horses before I even heard the reports. One of the horses, the one bearing the killer's body, broke loose and bucked forward toward the place the flashes had appeared. A couple of more shots racketed and the horse went down.

Lu's horse had folded silently, dead before he hit the ground. She dropped behind him, and, resting her gun arm on his side, fired a couple of shots at the hidden Apaches.

There was a bend in the canyon floor back about a hundred yards. Dragging my horse, the one carrying Paddock and the packhorse, I sprinted for that bend. If they got all our horses and left us afoot, our deaths would be assured.

I rounded the bend, immediately dropping the reins of my horse. I ran to Paddock, cut the rope that bound his feet together beneath the horse's belly, then said in an angry whisper, "Get off quick before I yank you off."

He was slow getting off so I yanked him off with the rope around his neck. He sprawled on the sand, unable to curse me because of the gag in his mouth. I yanked the rope again and he got up quickly and shambled after me to where Lu was, lying behind the dead horse. Paddock wasted no time getting down, and I flopped down between him and Lu. Paddock had hurt his broken arm falling and he was groaning with the pain. With the end of the rope that was around his neck, I tied his good hand, then went on to tie both his feet in a knees-bent position, drawn up against his rump. It was a cruel position and I knew how much pain he was in, but right at that moment I didn't give a damn. He'd inflicted worse pain on Lu time and time again. He'd murdered at least half a dozen men, maybe more, for the few material things they possessed. He had given our presence away to the Apaches, which had resulted in this attack, and I knew he'd kill me as quick as he'd step on a scorpion if he ever got the chance.

Lu said, "They will climb the hillside and get behind us. Or they will fire down on us."

We had three horses left and there were three of us alive. Suddenly, three guns fired in succession ahead of us.

Time was running short. If there were now only three Apaches firing at us from ahead, it meant four had climbed the slopes, two on each side. In a few minutes they'd be behind us. They'd have our horses and supplies.

I said, "Next time they fire, I'm going to rush them. I'm counting on those being single-shot guns. I figure I can get all three before they can reload. While I'm doing that, you go back and get the horses. Get the canteens out of the panniers but throw the panniers themselves away. Keep the gunnysacks. Can you do that?"

"I can do it."

I heard a rock dislodged up on the slope to my right,

but still ahead of me. At the same time, all three rifles roared nearly in unison.

I was on my feet before the reports had died away. Revolver in hand, I sprinted along the sandy bottom of the ravine. Behind me I could hear Paddock making desperate, protesting sounds behind the gag. He figured the Apaches wouldn't kill him if they recognized him, since he was married to Lu, but in the darkness they wouldn't recognize him and because of the gag he'd be unable to cry out.

I ran recklessly, knowing exactly how long it took to reload one of those old smoothbore guns. I saw a rock looming in the middle of the ravine, and saw movement behind it. A man raised up and I fired. He flopped backward as if I'd hit his breastbone. The other two raised up, split to right and left and tried to scramble up the hill.

There was not much light, only that from the stars and from a thin crescent moon. But the sand covering the bottom of the ravine was almost white and the dark figures of the Apaches showed up plainly enough for me to take aim and shoot.

One went down writhing with pain, but the other dropped and lay completely still. I didn't waste time finishing off the wounded one. I knew Lu needed me. I turned and sprinted back in the direction I had come from.

I could see her horse lying dead in the bottom of the ravine. There was only one figure behind the horse, and already the Apaches on the hillside were shooting down at it. Paddock yanked the gag out of his mouth and roared something in the Apache tongue.

I didn't even slow down. I didn't particularly want him killed. I wanted him to hang for his crimes, but right now there wasn't time for him. I ran on. A gun roared on the hillside and a geyser of sand picked up immediately in front of me.

Then I saw Lu coming, riding the packhorse bare-backed, leading mine, with the reins of the one Paddock had been riding tied to my saddle horn. The gunnysacks were slung over her horse's back in front of her.

Reaching her, I snatched the reins of my horse out of her hand and ran back to where Paddock was. With my fingers trembling, I untied his feet. Bullets slammed into the carcass of the dead horse and splatted into the sand. To Lu I said, "For God's sake, tell them who you are! You could get hit."

She didn't make a sound. She had renounced them, and besides, I supposed it wouldn't do much good now to identify herself. She was allied with their enemies and at least two of their number were dead because of it.

I got Paddock untied and whispered, "Get mounted and do it quick!"

I didn't have to urge him. His calling out to them in Apache, his identifying himself, had done no good. They wanted our horses and our guns, and besides, they wanted to avenge the two I had killed and the third I had wounded and maybe killed.

Lu sat her horse in the middle of the ravine as if she was sitting in the middle of the main street of Alkali Flat. I knew she wouldn't go until I did. As soon as Paddock was settled in his saddle I grabbed the rope that was still around his neck and mounted my horse. To Lu I whispered urgently, "Go! I'm right behind!"

She drummed her heels against the sides of the horse and he broke into a lope. There were a few more shots, but none came close. One struck a rock and ricocheted away whining into the distance.

We had the Apaches behind now but that didn't mean we were through with them. I waited until Lu slowed enough to let me range up close behind and then I yelled, "What will they do now? I killed at least two of them."

She was silent a few moments, apparently thinking it over. At last she said, "They may return to their camp, feeling that their medicine is bad. Or they may bury their dead, send the wounded one back to camp and come after us. Their guns are all very old. They would like to have the repeating guns we have and they are probably willing to risk a lot to get them."

It was still very hot in the bottom of this ravine. Well over a hundred, I would have guessed. I was soaked with sweat from the exertion and excitement of the fight. I laid a hand on my horse's neck and found it soaked as well. I said, "I think we'd better slow down."

She pulled her horse in immediately to a leisurely trot. This gait was excruciatingly painful to Paddock's broken arm and he protested loudly but I didn't care. Only when he began to curse both me and Lu did I turn my head. "Shut up or the gag goes back in."

He answered me with an obscenity. I halted my horse and got down. To Lu I asked, "Can you spare some more cloth?"

There was amusement in her voice as she replied, "I suppose so." She dismounted and knelt and I heard the sound of tearing cloth.

I wasn't satisfied with the way Paddock was secured anyway. I made him dismount, then removed the loop of the lariat from around his neck.

I ordered him to mount, then tied his feet underneath

the horse's belly with the hondo end of the lariat. I mounted, and, riding close, half-hitched it around his neck. There was still enough of it for me to hard-tie it to my saddle horn.

Lu handed me the strips of cloth she had torn from her petticoat. I moved my horse close to Paddock. He took a swing at me with his good hand. I avoided it. I said, "Do something like that once more and you'll finish the trip belly down on your saddle."

After that, he submitted to having the gag rammed into his mouth and tied in place. The intensity of his fury and hatred was almost tangible.

With Paddock securely tied and the gag in place once more, we moved out again. This time, Lu held her horse to a walk.

I'd lost the body of my prisoner, but I still had the money he had stolen from Satterfield and I'd trailed him to his grave so there could be no doubt about his identity.

And I had in custody an even worse murderer. But I wished to God I had some help. I wished Mr. McCabe was with me. A lot of miles of hot and hostile country lay between me and Alkali Flat, miles I couldn't begin to manage without some help.

I suddenly wished I understood Apaches better than I did. And I wished I understood women better than I did.

Lu had stayed two years with Paddock, enduring his abuse, watching while he murdered at least half a dozen men. That added up either to a sense of duty or to feelings of fear. Or maybe it added up to a wife's loyalty.

I'd have to be on guard until I was completely sure of her. Because if Paddock ever got loose, the first thing he'd do would be to kill me in the most painful way possible.

CHAPTER 6

The bottom of the ravine was dark, but the sand that covered it was white and reflected the starlight and that of the crescent moon, which soon would set behind the ridges to the west. There might not be enough light to see faces, but there was plenty for traveling. Besides, the horses' eyesight was a hell of a lot better than ours.

Lu let her horse plod on at a walk. I followed with Paddock's tied horse keeping pace. The horses were still lathered, and breathing hard, but they'd cool in half an hour or so at this gait.

I remembered sitting in Marshal McCabe's chair only two days ago, fingering the deputy marshal's badge I'd pinned to my shirt and admiring it and thinking how great it was going to be when I was a real deputy. Maybe I wasn't a deputy yet but I sure as hell was doing the work of one. Or trying to. I wondered if I was going to be able to bring it off, whether I'd be able to get Lu and Paddock and myself safely back to Alkali Flat with the money intact that had been in Satterfield's safe.

I'm not much given to self-doubt. I'm big and strong and I've always been able to handle most anything that came up. But suddenly I realized that I was only eighteen years old and that's a hell of a long way from being a grown man. I knew what hard work was, and I'd had some fistfights, but I'd never really been called on to do a man's work or accept a man's responsibilities.

Then I thought of Lu. She was even younger than I was, but she was a woman grown. She faced life and whatever it brought to her unafraid, with a kind of fatalistic belief that if things worked out and she survived, fine. If they didn't—well, she had done her best. I supposed that was the kind of attitude I ought to adopt. It seemed to have worked for her.

Yet it didn't seem to have embittered her and it hadn't turned her hard and bitchy the way some women get. I guessed that when I got married, if I ever did, I wanted a woman like her.

Suddenly I was comparing Lu and Sue Ann and getting more confused all the time. And then a thought hit me that hadn't occurred to me before. Lu wouldn't go back to the ranch after Paddock was executed and she couldn't go back to the tribe. Maybe her and me . . .

I muttered a curse underneath my breath. I was thinking crazy now, as if the heat was getting me.

We traveled for about an hour more. I put a hand down and felt my horse's neck. It was dry, but the hair was stiff with his dried sweat. I called out softly, "I think we can stop now for a little while."

She halted immediately. I dismounted and so did she, but I let Paddock remain on his horse.

We had lost the packhorse with his packsaddle and panniers back where we'd engaged the Indians. Gone were the oats I'd brought along to feed my horses. So were all the provisions. The two canteens had also been lost.

I dug the canteen Lu had brought from Paddock's ranch out of one of the gunnysacks slung across her horse's back, uncorked it and offered her a drink. She shook her head. "No. We may need it later more than we need it now."

I also abstained from taking a drink and I didn't even offer Paddock one. He made some muffled sounds behind the gag, and raised his good hand to try and yank it off. I said, "You do that and I'll tie your good hand so you can't use it either. Neither of us has had a drink and you don't get one either." I realized that the gag had probably made his mouth feel drier than ours but to tell the truth I didn't care. Let him be uncomfortable. It would be nothing to the discomfort Lu still was suffering from her battered face.

I poured a little water into my hand and moistened the mouths and nostrils of all three horses. They wanted a drink and kept trying to get at the canteen, but I kept it out of their reach.

I put the canteen back into the gunnysack. I loosened the cinches on the horses and untied the ropes that bound Paddock's feet under the horse's belly. He mumbled something behind the gag, probably a request for help in dismounting, but I ignored him. Lu sat down and put her back against a rock. I sat down facing back in the direction we had come, just in case the Apaches did the unexpected and caught up with us. Paddock paced back and forth, trying to get the circulation going again in his legs. I kept one eye on him but he didn't try anything.

We rested for about half an hour. The Apaches didn't come although I knew they'd have little trouble tracking us even in the dark. They'd be along in the morning, but by then maybe we'd be a long ways from here.

Finally I got up and told Paddock to mount. He did, for once not grumbling beneath his gag. I tied his feet underneath the horse's belly, careful in case he tried to kick out at me again. He didn't. Maybe he was waiting for a better chance. He knew now that even if he overpowered me, he still had to cope with Lu, who had a gun and had let him know earlier that she'd use it if necessary.

She mounted and I did, and we went on. I figured if we traveled all the rest of tonight, leaving this draw sometime during the middle of the night, we could find a place on a high ridge to hide and rest during the heat of the coming day. The Apaches could track us, of course, with no difficulty. But on high ground, with good cover, we'd be a match for them.

We found no good place to leave the ravine, though, and when gray first began to streak the eastern sky, we reached a place where some scrubby trees grew out of the bank at the side of the ravine. Even to my untutored mind, trees meant water. I said, "Let's stop here and see if we can't dig down deep enough to find water."

Lu had apparently had the same idea because she was already off her horse. After untying his feet I told Paddock to dismount. I pointed to one of the trees, and when he reached it, I tied his feet on one side of the tree trunk, then brought the rope around and tied his good hand to his feet, tight enough to give him no freedom or opportunity to get things untied.

Lu had a long-bladed hunting knife and was already digging, loosening the sand with the knife, then scooping it out with her hands. The hole she was digging was more than three feet across, which told me she expected the water to be deep.

After a while I took over, and we spelled each other for the better part of an hour. It was pleasant being close to her. What remained of her dress and petticoat failed to hide the very womanly curves of her body. Her hair was shiny and fine and black, and her face, now showing little swelling and only some scabs, was nice. There was sometimes humor in her eyes as she looked at me, and I supposed she was aware of the way I had been watching her. I hoped her humor wasn't mocking because of my age, but I didn't see how it could be because she was younger than I was.

Paddock watched us, scowling. Finally, two feet down, we hit damp sand, and about a foot farther struck water. Lu said, "We can stop now. The hole will fill."

We stopped. My hands were sore, but I knew hers were sorer still. We rinsed the sand off our hands and I saw that her fingernails were bleeding and the ends of her fingers raw.

I raised my glance from her hands. Her eyes were resting on my face with a strange expression as if nobody had ever bothered to care about her hurts before. We got up and stepped back away from the hole. Paddock's eyes were on me, knowing and threatening and mocking all at once. My face still felt hot and I knew it was flaming. That made me angry so for several moments I met his glance, giving him back venom for venom.

Unspoken though it might be, there was something tangible between Lu and me now. Something we recognized. She knew I wanted her and realizing that, I felt a surge of excitement like nothing I had ever experienced when thinking about Sue Ann Satterfield.

Slowly the hole filled with water. It was muddy at first, but we kept the horses away from it and gradually it cleared. I took the gag off Paddock long enough to let him drink his fill from the canteen. Then I replaced it. I handed the canteen to Lu and she drank sparingly. I drank myself, stopping before I had quite as much as I wanted. Then I knelt and refilled the canteen from the water at the bottom of the hole.

I let the hole refill, then led the horses to it, one by one. They had to get down on their knees to reach the water, but all of them drank like they were never going to stop.

Paddock went to sleep almost immediately, and I marveled at the human conscience that would let a systematic murderer like Paddock sleep like a baby as if there were nothing at all on his mind.

I didn't dare to sleep. Lu laid down and closed her eyes, and in a few minutes was breathing in the slow, deep manner of a person sound asleep.

Now, I was able to study her face and figure, openly and with no fear of the embarrassment of discovery. She was about five feet three, I guessed. Her body was strong yet its strength was not apparent. The curves of it were sweet and womanly, and her face, relaxed by sleep, seemed to me to be more beautiful than that of any woman I had ever seen.

I recalled that, during the beating at Paddock's ranch and subsequently during the dangerous and grueling trek from there to here, not once had her expression shown even the mildest form of irritation, anger or resentment. She was truly what she seemed to be, a woman who accepted without complaint whatever life bestowed on her.

However I tried not to, I couldn't help comparing her again to Sue Ann Satterfield. Lu's face was that of a mature, very beautiful woman, with warmth despite her experiences with Paddock and with a serenity that I felt could not, would not, be destroyed by anything. This was a woman who, even in my extreme youth, I realized I should not let slip away from me.

Which meant I couldn't kill Paddock, no matter what, because that would make any future with Lu impossible. But taking him in to be tried and convicted and hanged would place no obstacle between us.

And she seemed to like me well enough. At least the way I watched her hadn't offended her. She'd even seemed pleased by it.

She must have sensed me watching her, because her eyes opened, turned and met mine straight on. She smiled.

I groped for the things an eighteen-year-old might say, then discarded all of them and said what I really felt. "You are a very pretty woman."

"A married woman. Mr. Paddock may be executed, but he has not been yet."

I said, "I know." She was effectively stopping things. But I wouldn't be stopped. I asked, "How do you feel about me?"

I held my breath while I waited for her answer. Finally she said, "You seem older than your years."

"Is that all?"

She glanced at Paddock, apparently to be sure he was asleep. Then she said, "I am a squaw. An Apache squaw. There can be no future for you with me. A United States marshal cannot have a squaw."

I said, "Nobody said I had to be a United States marshal. There are a million other things that I can do."

"No matter what they are, in Arizona Territory you will be known as a squaw man. You might be accepted by the men but I would never be accepted by their womenfolk."

What she said was true. I had long cherished the dream that one day I would be a U.S. marshal's deputy and later, when I was older, U.S. marshal. I would have, could have, accepted being sheriff of a county or even marshal of a town. But my mind, young and inexperienced as it was, had long ago locked itself into the idea that my life would be spent enforcing the law.

I said, "I don't care." I knew even as I said it that it did not ring true.

Her smile was faint and sad. "But you do. You want to be a lawman. You have wanted that for as long as you have been able to think about such things."

"I can change."

"You don't know me. I am only another Apache squaw. I will go back to San Carlos and some Apache man will take me for his wife. I will have many children and will grow fat and old."

I felt anger suddenly. "Damn it, why are you trying to talk me out of it? I ain't going to say I'm in love with you because I don't know you well enough. But I could. And maybe I will. And if you get to feel the same way, it don't make no difference at all to me what I do. I can ranch. I can drive stage. And I ain't convinced that being married to an Indian will keep me from being a marshal or at least a marshal's deputy."

Paddock stirred and opened his eyes. He looked at the two of us blankly and I knew he had overheard nothing. But the conversation with her was over and its ending was unsatisfactory, at least to me. Nothing had been settled, or changed.

I looked at Paddock, then at Lu. I said, "Tell me about them all. About every man he killed. I want him to hear you telling it. I want him to know that I know and I want him to know that he is going to be tried for every one, that a hangman's noose is all he can look forward to."

"Where shall I start?" The reluctance in her voice was very noticeable.

I relented. "Never mind. It will all come out at his trial." There was no use in putting her through the ordeal of remembering each of half a dozen brutal murders, in which she had probably, afterward, been forced to participate. To the extent of helping him bury them at least.

The way she looked at me repaid me for relenting. I knew right then and there that I was going to have this woman if I could. If they called me "squaw man" to hell with them. If we had to, we'd go to California, or Oregon, or someplace where such things didn't matter anymore.

I studied her face as she watched Paddock's. And I saw something I had not seen before.

She was deathly afraid of him. She believed him to be able to do anything he set out to do, including escape, including the murder of both me and her. She had no hope for us. And she didn't want me to nurture hope.

She glanced at me, her eyes seeming to tell me one thing as plainly as if she had spoken it in words. Despite her earlier reminder that she was Paddock's wife, anything between the two of us must happen in the next few days. Because after that she firmly believed we both were going to be dead.

I could feel my blood running fast and hard within my head. The more I thought about it, and the more I watched her, the more I wanted her.

When you're eighteen and wanting is so strong in you, it's not an easy thing to wait. But I'd have to wait. Because I wasn't thinking about her as a squaw, to be bedded and forgotten. I was thinking in terms of permanence no matter how she tried to discourage me.

Whatever happened, I didn't want to hurt her. She had already been hurt enough.

CHAPTER 7

The air in the bottom of the ravine was like that in an oven. A few flies buzzed around us, but mostly they stayed near the horses. The horses kept switching at them with their tails, sometimes shaking their heads with an accompanying rattle of bits and the rings on bridle reins.

I closed my eyes against the glare and I must have dozed off. I awoke with a start and glanced immediately toward the place where Paddock had been.

He was still there, still trussed with one of his feet on one side of the scrubby tree, one on the other. His broken arm was held stiff and useless by the splint I had put on it, but in his good hand was a rock about five inches in diameter. His arm was drawn back to throw it at me.

What he would do if he managed to hit me with it and knock me out, I didn't know. Maybe he hadn't thought it through that far. As I sat up straighter preparatory to making an attempt to get out of the way, he flung the rock, with a deep growling sound in his throat, muffled by the gag.

The rock missed me by at least three feet due to the fact that his good arm, as well as his legs, was tied. He made more muffled sounds of anger and frustration beneath the gag but I wasn't paying any attention to him. I was looking for Lu, who had disappeared.

I got up and circled the bottom of the ravine, looking for her small footprints. I found them, heading south.

I followed for about half a mile and then turned back. I knew she hadn't run off and left us. She was simply scouting the land to the south, trying to find out what we could expect when we began traveling again.

I got the canteen, walked to Paddock and yanked the gag out of his mouth. I gave him a drink, pulling the canteen away before he'd drunk his fill. I picked up the gag preparatory to replacing it. He said, "I'll keep quiet. Just leave that damn thing out."

"Sure. You'll keep quiet just like you did before. Huh uh. It goes back in."

"She's run off and left us. You know that, don't you?"

"She'll be back. She's just scouting."

"Like hell! You don't know that redskinned bitch the way I do."

I stuffed the gag angrily into his mouth. He tried to bite my hand as I did and when he failed at that, he took a swing at me with his good arm. It struck the side of my head with considerable force, knocking me to the ground. I said, "You don't learn very damn fast. You'll wait for a drink next time until you figure I'm doing you a favor every time I give you one."

He glared at me. I finished with the gag, ready to hit him in the mouth if he took another swing at me. He didn't.

I went back and sat down, after taking a drink from the canteen myself and refilling it from the hole we'd dug. I didn't know how long Lu was going to be gone. It didn't particularly matter because it was still a long time until sundown. But I couldn't help worrying about her until I realized that she was Apache: she had their skills in trailing and in concealing herself. She could speak their language if she was surprised. Her stature was slight and she was unmistakably a woman so they wouldn't just shoot her down from a distance.

An hour passed. Then I heard a faint scuff of sand and glanced up to see her coming up the bottom of the sandy draw. She glanced at Paddock, then came straight to me and knelt at my side. "I've been scouting. I went about three miles."

"See any tracks?"

"Many tracks. All of them very fresh."

"How many Indians? Have any idea?"

"Fifty at least."

For a moment that seemed to doom any chance we might have had to go on. We'd have to turn and go back. And without food I didn't know how long we'd last.

She said, "I went to the edge of the mountains. There is a flat about three miles from here and about two miles out on the flat there is a road."

Suddenly I felt relief. I knew that road. It branched off the Tucson–Alkali Flat road, then ran north past the San Carlos agency and Fort Chiricahua and ended at a gold mine and small settlement called Bosque Mimbrero, which translates into Willow Grove. I knew there was a stage station about halfway between the Tucson road and Bosque Mimbrero and I figured that was about where we ought to be right now. I asked, "Did you see any buildings? Like a stage station and corrals?"

She nodded. "That seems to be what the Apaches are interested in. It's almost straight out from the mouth of this little draw. It has a windmill."

I'd been to the place. They had a shallow well in the sandy draw out of which the windmill pumped water for the corral. Water for the way station came from another well under the building itself. I asked, "Anything going on? Are the Indians attacking the place?"

"There were a few shots fired. There is a stagecoach sitting on the road two hundred yards north of the stage station. One of the horses is dead. The others are gone."

I was thinking that if we could reach the stage station we'd have a lot better chance of surviving than we did out here alone. Even if we turned around and went back, and found another way of reaching Alkali Flat, we'd run the risk of bumping into roving Apache bands. They weren't all here laying siege to this isolated stagecoach way station.

I considered it a minute and finally said, "Do you think we ought to try reaching it? After it gets dark?"

"It depends on where the Apaches camp, I suppose. And how sure of themselves they are. If they post guards all around the place there's very little chance of getting through."

We were silent several moments and then she asked, "How many stagecoaches run along that road every week?"

"Two."

"What days?"

"Tuesday and Friday."

"And this is?"

I tried thinking back counting the days in my mind from the time the Satterfield store had been robbed. I decided today must be Sunday. That meant the coach sitting out there with one of its horses dead had been the Friday stage, returning here on Saturday and due to reach Tucson on Sunday. It had probably reached here about dusk last night. The Apaches had shot one of the horses. In the ensuing darkness, the passengers must have made it to the safety of the stage station, where they were now holed up.

"There will not be another stage until next Tuesday evening?" Lu asked.

"No."

"Then the Apaches will not be worried about being surprised. There will be no guards. We will probably be able to reach the stage station all right. First dark, I would say, should be the best. They will be building fires and thinking about something to eat."

"See anything else? Any people? Any other coaches?"

"No people. And no stagecoaches. But there was an Army ambulance drawn up beside the stage station."

That was even more encouraging. An Army ambulance meant that there had to be some soldiers present. The Army wouldn't send an ambulance a hundred yards from Fort Chiricahua without an escort of some kind.

I tried to remember what date it was. I couldn't recall, but I knew it was near the end of the month. The ambulance had probably been carrying a paymaster. With a four-man escort. They would all be well armed and now inside the stage station helping fight the Apaches off. Furthermore, a paymaster detail would be missed. The commandant at Fort Chiricahua, forty miles north, would send out a patrol to look for him if he was more than a couple or three days late.

It looked to me like all we had to do was reach the stage station and get inside. All the things the Apaches wanted, or most of them, were outside. Horses. Saddles. The loot from the stagecoach boot. They wouldn't be much interested in the provisions inside the stage station nor would they be interested in the people there. Not when killing them meant heavy losses to themselves.

The sun was now down below the ridge toward the west. I knew it would take us until first dark to reach the edge of the mountains even if we started right away.

I saddled the horses and tightened the cinches, with Lu helping me. I hung the gunnysacks across the back of Lu's horse, then went to where Paddock was. I was cautious but I guess not cautious enough. No sooner had I untied his good arm and untied both of his feet than he slewed around and, lying back, kicked out viciously at my head.

I saw the kick coming and was moving away as his booted feet struck and that was probably all that saved me from having a busted head. As it was, I was knocked ten feet, to sprawl out helplessly, partially stunned. Not stunned enough that I couldn't see him scramble to his feet and come toward me, yanking out the gag, a savage triumphant expression on his face.

I looked helplessly toward Lu, knowing I'd never get my senses back in time to prevent him from seriously damaging me.

She had the gun I had given her earlier in her hand and the click of the hammer coming back seemed louder than it ever had before. But Paddock didn't look at her. He just kept coming, meaning to stomp my head into the rocky ground.

Lu's voice was sharp as a buggy whip. "Stop or I'll shoot!" She had the gun raised to eye level and was holding the heavy piece in both hands to steady it. One eye was closed, the other sighting down the barrel.

Paddock laughed, "Put that gun down or I'll kick the hell out of you."

Lu didn't speak again. But Paddock stopped suddenly and stared unbelievingly at her face. He seemed to realize that she really would shoot and he knew at this range, with her holding the gun the way she was, she wouldn't miss.

The whirling was leaving my head. I got up, drew my own gun from its holster, and pointed it at Paddock. "Get on your horse."

Scowling, he shuffled to his horse. He mounted, his face twisting with the pain. I picked up the rope I'd tied him to the tree with and went to his horse. I got on the side with his broken arm, then made a loop to go around his feet. I said, "Make just one move and I'll yank you off by your broken arm."

He didn't move. Lu was trembling now as she held the revolver dangling at her side. It was probably the first time she had ever defied him.

I drew the loop tight around his ankles, then ran it through the cinch buckle. Holding the end, I got my own horse, mounted and rode close to him. I tied his good wrist, drawing the rope tight deliberately because my head was aching so badly I was almost blind. Then, before he knew what I was doing, I took a couple of quick half hitches around the wrist of his broken arm and drew them tight. I rode ahead and handed the rope to Lu. "Keep it tight. I want the gag back in."

The gag lay in the dirt and, because it was wet from Paddock's saliva, sand and dirt had stuck to it. I didn't even shake it out. I jabbed at Paddock's mouth with my knife. He opened it to accommodate the gag.

I went back and took the rope from Lu. "Let's go."

"Are you all right?" she asked.

"I've got a headache but I'll get over it."

Her horse moved out and she presented her back to me. Paddock was damned careful to keep up now that his broken arm was subject to movement every time there was a little strain on the rope.

We moved along down the flat bottom of the draw. It wound back and forth, with rocky, cactus-covered hills rising steeply on both sides. There wouldn't be any Apache lookouts on those hills, I thought, because they wouldn't be expecting trouble from this direction. They'd be watching the roads leading to the stage station from north and south. And maybe they'd be watching west, for reinforcements.

I was a little puzzled. Lu had said there were at least fifty Indians laying siege to the way station. Why? That was what puzzled me. If it was only horses they wanted, they could have left last night. They had probably already looted the stagecoach. But they were waiting, probably for reinforcements that would make capture of the way station easy and relatively cheap in terms of Indian lives.

They must know time was against them. The paymaster's detail would be missed. So would the stagecoach. Help for the beleaguered whites in the stage station would come from both north and south. And, though the Apaches couldn't know it, help would also be coming from this direction in the form of Marshal McCabe's posse from Alkali Flat.

Dusk crept over the land as the last orange glow faded from the few high, thin clouds. Here in the bottom of the ravine, it got dark quicker than on the hillsides.

At last we reached the edge of the mountains and could look out across the plain. As a precaution I hard-tied the rope securing Paddock to my saddle horn. Gagged and trussed as he was, I didn't think he'd risk galloping his horse out into the midst of the Indians, but I wasn't going to take the chance.

Sitting quietly there in the bottom of the draw, we all searched the land ahead for signs of Indian guards. We could see the stage station, dark, its windows shuttered and barred so that no light seeped through. We could see the stagecoach, less than a hundred yards away. Half a dozen campfires winked beyond the range of rifle fire on the other side of the stage depot.

But nothing moved on this side of the station even though we searched the land carefully for a long time.

CHAPTER 8

Finally I said, "All right. We'll go in. Paddock, I'm going to untie your feet because you'll have to get off quick. But the rope is going to be around your neck. If you try anything, I'll drag you all the way."

He was still gagged so he couldn't say anything and it was too dark to see the way he looked at me. Not that I had to see.

First thing I did was untie the halter rope of Paddock's horse from my saddle horn. I dismounted and cut the rope that tied his feet. I mounted again and, holding the rope that was around his neck, I handed him his horse's halter rope. To Lu I said, "You go ahead. You can't ride between us, and whoever brings up the rear is most likely to catch any bullets they may shoot at us."

I had to smile, imagining Paddock's expression after that. I looked at Lu. "Go in quick. I'll be right behind."

I secured the end of the rope that was around Paddock's neck to my saddle horn, tying it hard. Lu moved out at a trot, giving me time to position myself directly behind her. She speeded up to a lope and finally, by drumming her heels on her horse's sides, to a run. I stayed about thirty or forty feet behind.

It was eerie, riding toward a dark and deserted building this way. What if nobody was there? What if they wouldn't let us in? What if we had to stay out front, banging on the door and yelling until the Apaches shot us down?

But we were committed. We were two thirds of the way there before I began to see dark figures rising up ahead of us. Lu, always quick-thinking, called out a couple of dozen Apache words at them and they held their fire.

Then we were on them. I held my breath for Lu's safety but she was already through before they grouped themselves or fired the first shot.

The first shot struck my horse squarely in the chest and he went down as though he had been clubbed. He threw me clear and I rolled along the side of the building, halfway to the front corner before I stopped. I got up and ran, stunned and surprised, and rounded the corner yelling, "Open up. Quick!"

I hadn't thought about Paddock and even now, when I did think of him, I discovered I didn't give a damn what happened to him. He was tied hard to the saddle horn on my dead horse, and if his horse had overrun mine, which was likely, he'd been yanked out of his saddle by the rope around his neck. If it hadn't broken his neck, or tightened permanently and choked him to death, he'd be coming because he sure didn't want to be out there in the dark, unable to speak, with half a dozen trigger-happy Apaches.

As it turned out, I didn't give him enough credit. He'd yanked the gag out when we first started in. He'd got the rope off his neck the instant the Apaches showed themselves in the darkness ahead of us, had hit the ground running, and now came up behind me and grabbed at my Spencer rifle, which I'd had the foresight to pull out of its saddle scabbard when we began the run toward the stage depot.

But he only had one hand to work with and even though he tried to knee me in the groin, I held on to the Spencer. Then he tried grabbing my revolver out of its holster and I lost patience with him. Holding the Spencer in both hands, I slammed it squarely into his face.

The door behind me opened and I turned. Several men stood there, all with guns. They were hesitating about letting Lu in. The sight of my face changed their minds. Lu hurried in, I followed. Paddock brought up the rear, blood running from his nose down over his mouth and dripping from his chin. A voice said, "That one's hurt! My God, there's blood all over him and his arm's broken!"

I opened my mouth to tell them not to waste any sympathy on Paddock when suddenly he said, "Put a gun on that dirty little killer! He overpowered me and took my guns and badge! The little son-of-a-bitch has killed seven men. He's worse'n Billy the Kid!"

His words took them by surprise, but not me. I sidled along the wall away from the door, which someone had just slammed and barred, and got myself into a corner. I raised the Spencer and pulled the hammer back to full cock. I said, "Don't anybody do anything hasty. He's the one who's killed seven men—for their horses and guns and whatever else they had on them. Buried them at his ranch, thirty miles back. The things he took from them are—" I suddenly realized I'd forgotten all about the gunnysacks. I looked at Lu. She had them, resting on the floor at her side now because of their weight. I finished my sentence, "—in there. That Apache girl's his wife. Ask her which of us is the killer and which is the lawman."

There were about a dozen people in the room. They

looked first at Paddock, then at me, then at Lu, trying to make up their minds what was the truth. I said, "It's easy enough to prove. Look at Lu's face. Then look at that son-of-a-bitch's knuckles. He was beating her when I rode into their place a couple of days ago."

One of the men walked to Paddock, took his good arm and by sheer force turned it until he could look at Paddock's knuckles. They were skinned all right. I said, "Now look at mine." I stuck the Spencer under my arm, muzzle still pointing at the group, and then held out my hands, palms down. There wasn't a mark on my knuckles.

The man who had hold of Paddock's arm dropped it. He said, "If he's that bad, we'd better tie him up."

I nodded and lowered the barrel of the Spencer. I eased the hammer down to half cock and leaned the gun against the wall in the corner of the room.

A stocky man with a close-cropped beard that I guessed was probably the station agent because he seemed to know his way around better than the others, went into a closet at the rear of the room and came out holding a coil of rope. It was limber and just right for tying Paddock up, not stiff like a lariat.

I looked at Paddock. "Go over and sit down at the end of that long table. The far end."

"You go to hell."

I shifted the coil of rope into my left hand and drew my revolver with my right. Paddock said contemptuously, "You won't shoot me."

"Nope. But I'll sure lay this on the side of your head above your ear. Move!"

Sullenly he shuffled to the table. A man said, "That arm won't heal straight."

I didn't give a damn how it healed to tell the truth, but

I looked at the man who had spoken. He was short, white-skinned and soft. He had a three or four days' growth of whiskers and his eyes were red, the lids puffy over them. We had two drunks in Alkali Flat, one of them the veterinarian, so I knew the signs. I asked, "You a doctor?"

He nodded. "Phineas Scott, at your service."

I said, "Wait until I tie him up and then you can reset it."

"I haven't any laudanum."

"Then give him whiskey. Or hit him on the head. After all the trouble he's given me I don't care what you do with him."

I went to the table, where Paddock had found himself a place at the end. There was a crosspiece running between the legs. Both legs and crosspiece were oak and very heavy, hewed out by hand from what looked like a wagon's running gear. I said, "One leg on each side. Try to kick me and I'm going to let you have this gun barrel right in the mouth." I was out of patience with Paddock and I had no intention of taking any more punishment from him.

I tied Paddock's ankles together, as tight as I could. I didn't think the ropes would cut off the circulation but I didn't care. He submitted meekly, apparently believing me when I told him I'd rap him on the head with my gun if he gave me any more trouble.

When I got through with that, I looked at the pale, red-eyed drunk and said, "All right, reset his arm. Then I'm going to tie the other one."

The doctor disappeared into one of the small bedrooms that opened off the large main room of the station, and a moment later came back carrying a small black doctor's bag. He asked the stationmaster, the stocky one with the trimmed beard, if he had a straight stick, not too thick, that could be used as a splint. He said he needed two if possible.

The man disappeared and a little later came back with two thick oak yardsticks. "You can use these but I want 'em back."

The doctor took the yardsticks. He was already unwinding the bandage from Paddock's arm. He was very careful with the last few layers so as not to let the bone ends slip out of place. He glanced at me. "You did a good job of setting it."

Paddock's face was pale, and for once he wasn't glaring at anybody. His other hand had gripped the edge of the table so hard his knuckles showed white.

The doctor asked somebody to bring him a drink and I could see why he needed one. His hands were shaking uncontrollably. The stationmaster brought him a bottle and he must have drunk half a pint before he took it away from his lips. He waited a moment, drank some more, then put the bottle down on the table and went to work again. He reset the arm and began to rebandage it using the same bandages he had taken off the arm. There wasn't anything wrong with them except for some blood and quite a bit of dirt. He put the clean part next to the arm.

He finished and tied the ends of the bandage, then took another drink from the bottle. He gave Paddock what was left of the whiskey. Paddock drank it and then growled, "You son-of-a-bitch, I needed that worse than you did."

I moved in and took the bottle away from Paddock before he could hit somebody with it. I tied his good arm down at his side, tight. I said softly, "You use any abusive language or try to talk anybody into turning you loose and I'll gag you again."

For the first time, I looked around the room, really noticing the people there. There was the doctor, who had found another bottle someplace and was sitting in a rocking chair holding it in his lap.

There was the stationmaster, stocky, his beard trimmed short. There was a competent look about the stationmaster, which wasn't surprising. He ran this way station all by himself, without even the help of a wife, although there was an Indian woman, as stocky as he was, who pretty much stayed out of the way. I gathered she was his kitchen help. Lu went over and began talking to her in Apache. A few of the white people stared at the two suspiciously, as if by speaking in an unfamiliar language they were putting us all in jeopardy.

The stationmaster called, "Why don't all of you gather around and we'll get acquainted."

The people moved in slowly toward the stationmaster. He asked me, "What's your name, son?"

"Jason Cole."

"You're young for a deputy."

I don't know what it was that kept me from telling him the truth. An instinct for self-preservation, I suppose. Nobody was going to listen to an eighteen-year-old boy. And furthermore, my story that I was the marshal and Paddock the prisoner was going to lose credence if they knew I was only wearing the badge. To change the subject as quickly as possible, I said, "The prisoner is Nathan Paddock." I nodded toward Lu. "She's his wife. Her given name is Luisa. She said her Apache name was too hard for white people to pronounce so the agent at San Carlos gave her the name of Luisa."

The people acknowledged the introduction to Lu if not to Paddock. The stationmaster said, indicating the lieutenant, "This is Lieutenant Wolcott. He's head of a paymaster detail headed for Fort Chiricahua. The troopers are Sergeant Riley, Private Duran and Private Cantrell." The three troopers were still at the front windows, not able to see out because of the light inside the room and the shutters, but ready in case the Apaches tried to storm the place. They turned and ducked their heads in acknowledgment.

Lieutenant Wolcott was a tall, thin man, darkened by the Arizona sun but with a mark of inexperience on him that was unmistakable. I remember wondering why the hell anybody would send a paymaster detail through Apache country with an inexperienced man in charge.

The stationmaster said, "I'm Donovan and the Injun woman is Belle."

I asked, "What are the Indians after? Don't seem logical they'd attack a place with this many men defending it unless they had a powerful reason for doin' it."

He glanced at me a little more sharply than before. Then he said, "Gold. The Apache never did agree to that settlement at Bosque Mimbrero but at the time there wasn't much they could do because the Army had 'em all herded into the reservation at San Carlos. When they thinned the Army out, bands of 'em started breakin' away. They attacked Bosque Mimbrero five nights ago. Killed everybody but these few folks here and burned the place to the ground. Stage got away just in time. The driver's Litzo and the guard is Axleford. The lady is Flo and the other four are miners, Pacheco, Ramsey, Silva and Mock."

A middle-aged woman was sitting quietly on a hard-cushioned sofa on the side of the room. Donovan noticed the direction of my glance and said, "That's Miss Moffatt. The boy, Jess, is her nephew. They were headed for Bosque Mimbrero to see the boy's father and try to get him to come home. That stage driver heard there was trouble and wouldn't go on. Left 'em stranded here because they wouldn't go with him when he went back."

That left only two men, rough-looking characters you wouldn't turn your back on if they rode into your camp at night. Donovan said, "One of them, the light-haired one, calls himself Beechner. The other's Yorty. They were headed for Willow Springs and got stranded here when the stage went back."

Now I knew who everybody was. The lieutenant and the four troopers could fight. I could, and so could Donovan. The four miners could and so could the drifters. The driver and shotgun guard of the stage that had stopped here on the way from Willow Springs to Tucson could also fight.

That made fifteen men, not counting the doctor, who, if he kept on the way he was going now, would be too drunk to shoot a gun.

But outside there were fifty or sixty Apaches. Waiting. Waiting either for dawn or for reinforcements to come. Maybe for both.

I asked Donovan, "Why do the Indians want that gold so bad? I thought Indians didn't care about it."

He shrugged. "They don't care about it, for itself. But they know it will buy rifles and ammunition and horses. Besides that they want our guns. And they probably want the women."

Well, there it was. I'd thought I had trouble getting Paddock back to Alkali Flat, but I hadn't known what trouble was. Even if Marshal McCabe arrived with a posse, it wouldn't be big enough to fight more than fifty hostiles. And if the commandant at Fort Chiricahua sent out a patrol to look for the paymaster, it probably wouldn't consist of more than a dozen men.

Nope, we were on our own. Maybe I'd never get to wear a marshal's star, or even, legitimately a deputy's badge. But I reckoned that when you picked being a lawman as what you wanted to do with your life, you had to take the bad with the good.

CHAPTER 9

As soon as I found out the Apaches were after the money inside the way station, I decided I had better try getting out, along with Lu and the money in the gunnysacks. This bunch of people weren't going to be able to fight off fifty or sixty Apaches. They were sure to lose. Come daylight, the Apaches would find some way of setting the place afire, and after that it would only be a matter of time.

And I sure as hell didn't intend to let a bunch of Indians have the money from the Alkali Flat store just to buy guns from some crooked white gunrunner. I figured I had to get it out of the stagecoach station before daylight. On the other hand, I couldn't see myself riding back to Alkali Flat without even thinking about the fate the people inside the way-station building faced.

That left me only one alternative. I had to get out, all right, tonight, and I had to take the money with me. But I couldn't go straight to Alkali Flat with it. Plain decency required that I go first to Fort Chiricahua and alert the commandant, so that instead of sending a four- or six-man patrol to look for his paymaster, he'd send a force large enough to defeat the Indians besieging this place.

Lu was across the room, talking softly with the fat Apache woman who helped Donovan run the place. I walked to her and said, "I want to talk to you."

She spoke a few swift words to the Apache woman, then followed me to a corner of the room. I said, "This place is going to be overrun tomorrow. When it is, all that money from Alkali Flat is going to be taken. I figure I've got to get out of here tonight with it. I figure on going to Fort Chiricahua to let the commander know what's going on here, and then heading back to Alkali Flat. Will you come with me?"

She showed no hesitation of any kind. She simply nodded, as if the question had been foolish and unnecessary.

The gunnysacks were in my possession now. I said, "We can't go until everybody's settled down for the night."

She nodded silently. She returned to the Indian woman. The two began to talk again. She seemed to enjoy the company of Belle.

Carrying the gunnysacks, I walked to a rough, homemade bench and sat down to wait. Beechner and Yorty, the two drifters, approached me and Yorty, the shorter of the two, asked, "How much money you got in them gunnysacks?"

I asked, "What business is that of yours?"

He bristled. "What's the matter with *you?* You got some idea that we're going to try robbing you? Where would we go, with all them Apaches outside? What we're worried about right now is savin' our scalps."

I said, "I've got the money Paddock stole from the men he killed, which isn't a hell of a lot. I've got some guns and personal effects and that's all. If you want to try killing me for that, go right ahead. But it isn't worth your while. If you want something worth your pains, try the paymaster or those miners that are keeping such a close watch on their gold."

Yorty said, "You're a smart-alec kid. Didn't nobody ever tell you to show some respect for your elders?"

It was stupid, but I said it anyway. "Age don't make a man. You two could be a hundred and you'd still be a couple of vultures."

Beechner said, "You smart little bastard! I ought to take some of that sass out of you."

I said, "Anytime. Right now, if that's what you want."

"I can wait."

Maybe it was stupid to egg Beechner and Yorty on, but I'd wanted them to get one thing straight from the start. I wasn't afraid of them. And there wasn't any way they could know whether the money I had was worth their while or not. What I really wanted to plant in their minds was the idea that it would pay them a lot better to try for the Army payroll or for the gold the miners were guarding so carefully. I was willing to bet they had two or three times as much as I had.

Beechner and Yorty had hardly gotten out of earshot when the lieutenant approached. He asked, "How's everything?"

"All right."

"Mind answering a few questions for me?"

I shrugged. If anyone had authority here it was either him or me or maybe both of us.

He asked, "What were you doing all alone when you happened onto Paddock's place?"

I wasn't too anxious to give away the fact that I had all the money from Alkali Flat, but I figured if I couldn't trust this Army officer I couldn't trust anyone. I said, "The store was robbed in Alkali Flat while I was watching the marshal's office. Mr. Satterfield, who ran the store, had a safe and kept money for the townspeople. The robber cleaned out the safe and killed Mr. Satterfield. Since the marshal wasn't there, I figured it was up to me to trail him and I couldn't get nobody else to go with me. By the time I'd trailed him to Paddock's ranch, Paddock had already killed and buried him. I dug him up and was going to pack him in, but we ran into some Apaches and they got some of our horses. I know about where the body is, though."

"Then you've got a substantial amount of money in those gunnysacks. You'd better watch them pretty carefully."

"I figure to. Just about as close as you're watching your payroll chest."

I seemed to have satisfied him for the moment at least because he walked away and rejoined his trooper escort on the far side of the room. I noticed that they all carried sidearms and a couple of the troopers had Spencer rifles besides. I doubted if Beechner and Yorty would try for the payroll or for the gold. Both were too well guarded. What they'd go for would be my gunnysacks because I was all by myself and just a kid.

Only I wasn't going to be here. That was what they couldn't know.

I let myself relax, keeping one foot on the gunnysacks and keeping an eye on the two drifters. The firing outside finally died away as the Indians realized they were only wasting ammunition. Several people tried to make themselves comfortable, and a few dozed off. Finally Donovan went around the room blowing out the lamps. He left one burning, on the table where Paddock was tied.

Everybody settled down. They all knew they'd have to be up before dawn, because at dawn the Apaches would attack.

Lu left the fat Apache woman and came to me. She sat down beside me. "When are we going?"

"We'll give 'em time to get to sleep. And the Apaches too, outside."

"The Apaches will have sentries. They will see us leave."

"I didn't figure it would be easy."

"We will not have horses."

I grinned a little. "I figured you could get some for us. You speak their lingo and in the dark they won't be able to tell you're a woman."

"They will be able to tell."

"Then we'll have to try getting you some men's clothes. Maybe we can jump one of the sentries."

She was silent after that, and from her silence I guessed it was a plan of which she could approve. She closed her eyes and seemed to go to sleep almost instantly. Her head sagged and rested on my shoulder, which was not at all unpleasant as far as I was concerned.

I knew I ought to sleep. I'd need it. I also knew I couldn't. I was too nervous and keyed up. Besides, if I slept, I might find the two gunnysacks missing when I woke up.

Sitting there, I tried to spot the position of everybody, particularly the two drifters, Beechner and Yorty. They had settled down to sleep about ten feet from the door, but each of them had a blanket and both were facing away from it. Either they were a lot slyer than I gave them credit for, or else they weren't worried about me trying to get away. I guessed the last was true. There was no reason for them to suspect I'd try to leave.

Somebody began to snore, and after a little while, somebody else began to snore. I'd been watching and for a long time nobody had moved more than just to roll over or shift position. I gripped Lu's arm and she awoke instantly with no sound. She lifted her head from my shoulder. I whispered, "It's time."

She sat there for a moment, her glance sweeping the room. I waited, knowing that if anything looked wrong, she'd spot it a whole lot quicker than I ever could. But apparently nothing was amiss, because she got to her feet. I stooped and picked up the gunnysacks, but she took them from me and slung them across her shoulder. By way of explanation, she touched my gun with her hand. What she meant was that I was going to have to do the fighting and the least she could do was relieve me of the burden of the gunnysacks.

We picked our way silently and slowly toward the door. I kept my eyes on Beechner and Yorty, but neither moved. I turned my head and looked at Paddock, knowing he'd give us away if he could. He appeared to be asleep.

As we passed Donovan asleep on the floor, he raised his head. "Damn fool."

I didn't reply. After a moment he said softly, "Good luck, kid."

I was grateful for that. We reached the door and still neither Beechner nor Yorty had moved. I raised the bar and cautiously opened it. It squeaked thunderously in the almost complete silence.

Paddock raised his head. Seeing us going out, he yelled, "Hey! The son-of-a-bitch is gettin' away!"

I slammed the door. I sure didn't want Paddock's yelling reaching the Apaches. I didn't give a damn if he woke up everybody in the stagecoach station. They weren't going to be following us anyway.

As silent and careful as two ghosts, Lu and I moved away from the building. It occurred to me that I wasn't being fair to Lu, risking her life this way. Left to her own devices, she could have escaped the way station easily in the darkness with no risk to her life. But she had given up her heritage the first time when she married Paddock and later when she chose to go with me. I couldn't force her to do anything she didn't want to do.

But I promised myself one thing. I'd never let her down. I wouldn't abandon her just because white people hated Apaches and would classify me as a "squaw man" because I was living with her or was married to her.

Behind me I could hear Paddock yelling. Then, suddenly, it was quiet in the way station and I wondered what had happened. We were about three hundred yards from the place when, glancing back, I saw a dim square of light appear. It disappeared almost instantly but not before I had guessed what it meant.

Beechner and Yorty were after us. They might even have brought Paddock with them, although wounded as he was that wasn't likely.

So we'd have to hurry. In our favor was the fact that Lu was Apache and could speak the language, and if we could get some men's clothing from a sentry, she would have no trouble in getting horses for us.

Beechner and Yorty, on the other hand, would find it almost impossible to steal two horses from the Indians. Unless they were more skilled than I thought they were, they'd make a racket the Apache horse guards couldn't miss.

But if they followed us they could get horses at the San Carlos agency. They'd be a long ways behind, but even so they could probably reach the fort before the commandant could get things under way.

About fifty yards from the way-station building, I stopped and stood absolutely still. Lu followed suit. Hardly daring to breathe, we both listened for some sound.

The chances were not good that the Apaches were unaware that someone had left the building, but I was hopeful that the Apache sentry might become careless and make a noise. If he had a horse with him, it was certain that sooner or later the horse would snort or move.

We must have stood virtually frozen for at least five full minutes. We could both hear the sounds being made by Beechner and Yorty between us and the way station. In a way that was good, in a way bad. They would alert the sentries. On the other hand, the sentries would not expect someone else to be between them and the men making the noise.

Finally I heard something beyond us in the darkness. At the same time I felt Lu's grip on my arm tighten. I drew my revolver, but I didn't cock the hammer because the last thing I wanted to do was fire it.

Like a shadow, Lu released my arm and faded into the darkness ahead. I followed her, only able to see her because she was moving. If she had not been, she would have been invisible.

I bumped into her when she stopped. She made no attempt to communicate with me. She just waited, silent and still, for me to see the sentry for myself.

It took me a couple of minutes to do so. Then I saw him, sitting on a rock. He didn't have a horse, which explained our not hearing one. I gripped Lu's shoulder and then, as silently and cautiously as I have ever moved in my life, I headed for the Indian.

The main thing, when I closed with him, was to avoid making a sound. I doubt if I had ever been more tense in my whole life. I was sure I'd killed at least one or two Apaches on the way here, but it hadn't been the kind of close hand-to-hand combat this encounter was going to be.

I glanced back once. Lu had crouched to the ground. She had a gun, but she'd be as unwilling to use it as I was to use mine.

The Apache was looking in the direction of the Indian camp, where the coals of a few fires still glowed. Against their reddish light, I could occasionally see Indians moving back and forth.

I speeded up, knowing my intended victim might turn his head at any instant. He probably wouldn't see me where I was now because he had been looking at a source of light, however dim. But if his head happened to be turned toward me when I closed with him . . .

Having decided this, I closed with a final rush, not as silently as I would have liked. His head snapped around and he made it halfway to his feet. Then my gun barrel descended on his skull with a very audible crack. I put a hand over his mouth as I struck and he sagged to the ground without a sound.

Lu was there immediately. I laid my gun aside and began stripping the few clothes the Apache wore from his body. I didn't bother with the high-topped moccasins because Lu had moccasins of her own. He had no pants, only a breechclout secured by a thong around his waist and leggings. He wore a thin cotton shirt that had undoubtedly been issued to him at the agency. He also wore a trooper's coat, of blue wool material with brass buttons and epaulets on the shoulders. It was badly worn and had a sour, sweaty smell.

While I undressed the sentry, Lu shed her own clothes. She stood entirely naked for a moment in the starlight before she began putting on the clothes I handed her. Seeing her that way almost made me forget the business at hand, but it didn't take her long to dress and I got my mind back on what we were doing here. She picked up the gunnysacks and handed them to me, along with her clothes, then disappeared into the darkness. I stuffed her clothes into one of the gunnysacks.

I stood there waiting, keeping an eye on the unconscious Apache sentry and listening for sounds from the direction of the way station. I heard nothing. Despite my determination not to, I began thinking about the way Lu had looked, standing there in the starlight. Her body had been blurred by darkness, but it had seemed very white and it had certainly been stirring. I don't know how long I waited. It seemed like half an hour at least although I knew it couldn't have been more than ten minutes. Finally I heard horses' hoofs, and a moment later she was beside me, the lead ropes of two horses in her hand.

She gave one to me. I slung the gunnysacks over the horse's back and swung astride. Lu was already mounted. With Lu leading and less than twenty feet apart, we moved north as silently as we could. I kept looking back, but there was no outcry and I saw nobody following us.

I wondered about Beechner and Yorty and where they were. Probably ahead. But Lu would see them, or her horse would, long before they saw us.

CHAPTER 10

As it turned out, Lu's horse was the first to spot the drifters. Lu halted him at the instant the horse's ears pricked toward them, and even before I could reach her, she had begun to turn the horse aside.

My horse closed quickly with hers at the instant a shot blasted directly ahead. I don't know whether Beechner and Yorty thought we were Indians or not. They probably did, because Lu was still dressed like an Apache and I had been too far behind her for them to see.

Without knowing whether she was hit or not, I gave her horse a cut across the rump with my rifle barrel and at the same time left the saddle and flopped down prone on the ground. Lu's horse sprinted away and my horse followed close behind.

I knew right off that this was a hell of a fix to be in. Beechner and Yorty thought I was an Apache. Worse, the real Apaches would have been awakened by the gunfire and would be coming this way as fast as their horses could carry them. I'd be right in the middle.

Ahead of me, an urgent voice said, "Get after 'em, for Christ's sake! Get the horses!"

Ahead of me, two figures rose up from the ground, visible only as shadows. I began firing with my Spencer and both dropped back immediately to the ground. There must have been three, because before they'd even hit the ground, three rifles were firing at me.

Bullets struck nearby rocks and ricocheted away into the night.

The first shots had been aimed at my muzzle flashes. I began backing and angling away, staying prone. It was urgent that I get clear of these three men immediately because there was going to be a swarm of Apaches all around us within a minute or two.

I got back about fifty feet before I dared to get up. Then I began running, as quietly as I could, in the direction Lu had gone.

I could hear the Apaches coming, their horses' hoofs thundering against the ground. I ran as hard as I've ever run for about three hundred yards before I saw the dim shapes of two horses ahead. I grabbed the lead rope of my horse from Lu and leaped astride, nearly missing the horse's back entirely because of the way the frightened animal danced away.

My inclination would have been to drum my heels against the horse's side and ride like hell, but Lu was thinking straighter than I was. At a walk, she rode her horse away from the scene. The thunder of horses' hoofs behind us stopped and sporadic rifle fire broke out. Looking back, I could see gun flashes from where the three white men were and, shortly thereafter, flashes from the Indians' guns.

I didn't know how it was going to come out, whether the white men, with their repeating rifles, would kill the Indians and get their horses or whether the Indians would surround the whites and wait them out.

I didn't care. What I cared about now was Lu. I ranged my horse up beside hers. "Are you all right?"

"Yes." But there was pain plainly apparent in her voice and I knew she had been hit.

Suddenly I was scared, more scared than I'd been fighting Paddock or facing Indians. If anything happened to Lu . . .

I said, "Stop. You've got to stop and let me take care of it." I was trying to make myself believe it was a minor wound. But down deep I was terrified that it was not.

She resisted stopping until I said, "They're back there nearly half a mile. We can take time to stop."

Maybe she would still have resisted me, but I reached out and took her horse's lead rope. I slid to the ground and she did too. I wanted to take care of her immediately but I knew the horses had to be secured first. Otherwise they'd go straight back to the Indian camp.

I found a thick clump of brush and tied both horses to it securely, then I turned to Lu. "Where are you hit?"

I held my breath, waiting for her reply. She leaned against me, apparently weakened by pain or loss of blood. In my mind I started to pray, "Oh, God . . ."

Then I heard her voice, a bare whisper. "My shoulder. It's bleeding pretty bad."

I grabbed her petticoat out of the gunnysack where I'd put it earlier. By feel, I ripped some strips from it, then carefully helped her remove the faded-blue cavalry jacket and the cotton shirt.

She was naked to the waist and I couldn't help being aware of that, but I was too concerned with her wound to let myself think about it. There wasn't much light, just that from the stars, but her skin was light for an Apache, and the blood was dark and very visible against it. I asked, "Can you move your arm?"

She did, without making a sound. I said, "All right, I

don't think the bullet hit a bone." I began wrapping strips of cloth around her shoulder after first putting a pad over the wound. In the darkness, it looked to me like a bullet gouge because there was only one wound, not two. And unless the bullet had hit a bone it would not have lodged in her shoulder and stayed.

But it was deep and, I knew, painful as hell, because it had torn the shoulder muscle and every movement she made must be agony. I finished and helped her with the shirt. "Can you ride?"

"I can ride." Her voice was so soft I could hardly hear.

I untied the horses and boosted her up on one of them. I mounted mine, holding the lead rope of hers. If she didn't have to guide the horse it would be a lot easier for her to favor her wounded arm and keep it from causing her so much pain.

The shooting behind us had died down to an occasional shot. Finally it stopped altogether. I didn't know whether the three whites had beaten the Indians or whether it was the other way around. Or they might still be fighting and we might simply have passed out of hearing.

To be on the safe side I had to assume that, with their repeating rifles and revolvers, the three white men had defeated the handful of Indians that had been sent against them. Which meant they might have horses. Which also meant they'd flee quickly before the main body of the Indians besieging the way station attacked.

They would be behind us, then. They'd come swiftly along this road until they believed themselves to be safe from Apache pursuit. Then they'd camp, and at daybreak would pick up our trail.

That was what I believed. But I was a hell of a long

ways from being sure of being right. I rode up beside Lu. "From the sound of it, I'd guess they've killed the Apaches and taken their horses. How is your shoulder? Do you think you can ride faster than a walk?"

"Yes."

I said, "A trot's going to be too hard on you. But an easy lope . . ."

"All right."

She was one hell of a woman, I thought. I could see that she had grasped the long hair of the horse's mane with both hands and was holding on. I was leading her horse so she didn't have to guide the animal. All she had to do was remain conscious and hold on to her horse's mane.

The gunnysacks were now lying across my horse's withers in front of me. I felt cruel and unfeeling, forcing her to ride, but I knew there was no other choice. I kicked my horse into a slow, rocking lope. The lead rope of Lu's horse tightened briefly, then slackened as her horse matched the pace of mine. I heard no sound from her, of pain or protest, and I somehow knew I never would. It is not only Apache men that are taught to bear pain stoically. The women receive the same teaching. I had heard that in childbirth an Apache woman is silent.

Finally, after we had traveled this way for more than an hour, I reined my horse aside toward a grove of cedars that I could see as a darker area against the hillside. I dismounted, went back and caught Lu in my arms as she slid limply from her horse. I left her standing while I secured both horses, each to a cedar tree. Then I returned to her.

She was swaying with weakness. The white bandage,

when I pulled back her shirt to look at it, was dark with fresh blood.

I said, "Come lie down."

She did not protest. I found a level place and helped her lie down. I got the gunnysacks and placed them under her head to serve as a pillow.

Then I returned to the horses. Even at night, the air temperature was above ninety. The horses were lathered and breathing reasonably hard, but they still had a lot of strength in them. I got the canteen, which had been secured to the gunnysacks. First I moistened Lu's lips. Then I poured a little into my hand and moistened the muzzles of the two horses. After that I returned to Lu and sat down beside her on the ground. I didn't dare to sleep, despite the fact that we were nearly a quarter mile off the road. Our horses might smell others passing, or others passing might smell ours and signal, and bring either Apaches or our hard-case pursuers down on us.

Beechner and Yorty knew, of course, that we had taken the road due north. They probably believed that we were headed for Fort Chiricahua to warn the commandant of the siege. But they could not be sure. And if they did not camp, if they galloped hard along that road all night, they might well find themselves miles ahead of us.

Lu breathed softly and regularly beside me and I knew she had either gone to sleep or passed out from the pain. I got up, walked to where the horses were tied, and untied one of them. I led it back to where Lu was sleeping and tied the halter rope around my wrist. I could doze now, even if I couldn't sleep. The horse would warn me if anybody came close, even if he could neither hear nor smell horses passing on the road.

I dozed, and dreamed I was chasing a gang of desperadoes all by myself. I dreamed of being alone with Lu, safe, sound and in love. I woke up with a start as the horse shook his head and yanked on my wrist.

I was fully awake before light began to touch the eastern horizon. I struck a match, opened the cover of my silver hunting-case watch and looked at the face. It was four o'clock.

I stirred Lu, taking care to shake her gently by her unhurt shoulder. She wakened immediately. I said, "I think we ought to go on. If those drifters kept traveling, they will have gone past by now."

I helped her to her feet. I boosted her on the horse, whose halter rope I had tied to my wrist and then, leading the animal, went after my horse. I mounted and we rode out at a walk.

I reached the road. Handing the halter rope of my horse to Lu, I dismounted. On hands and knees I inspected the surface of the road for tracks. There were a lot of old tracks, but only three sets of fresh ones, the tracks of unshod ponies traveling at a hard gallop north. Satisfied, I took the halter rope from Lu and mounted again.

I knew exactly what had happened now. Anxious to put distance between themselves and the Apaches, the three pursuing us had ridden hard, probably for ten or fifteen miles. They had found the tracks of Lu's horse and mine. And satisfied that we were, indeed, heading either for the San Carlos agency or Fort Chiricahua, they had remounted and gone on.

Which meant, to me, that they were now well ahead of us. Unless they stopped to inspect the road again, there'd be no reason for them to believe we were behind them. But if they did know they might be planning to ambush us.

Now, because of the need to be extremely watchful, not only for an ambush ahead but for scattered bands of Apaches, which seemed to be everywhere, I held our horses to a walk. The sky turned gray and finally the sky in the east turned pink as the rising sun stained a few thin clouds.

Lu's face seemed to have more color this morning and I knew the sleep had done her good. Her face, furthermore, was not as swollen as it had been yesterday, although the scabs where the skin had been broken by Paddock's blows were still there.

Our position was precarious and I feared for Lu's safety. I realized that if trouble did come the money in the gunnysacks would be a hindrance. I wished there was someplace I could hide the money.

CHAPTER 11

At about seven, we reached the road that led into the agency at San Carlos. I could see the tracks of the horses the three were riding plainly enough without dismounting because it was early and there had been no traffic on the road. There were no fresh tracks coming out of the agency.

I didn't have to point out the tracks or point out to Lu the fact that no tracks had left the agency. She had already noticed. I said, "It wouldn't hurt if we had fresh horses, some water, and a few provisions. Let's hide until they leave."

We rode off to one side of the road, finding no concealment until we reached the crest of a small knoll. We hid our horses behind it, then crept carefully to the top to watch.

We didn't have long to wait. The three appeared. Beechner in the lead, Yorty following and Paddock bringing up the rear. I was a little surprised to note that the bandage on his arm had not been changed, but he did have a dark piece of cloth tied around his neck to serve as a sling.

I asked, "Isn't there a doctor at the agency?"

Lu nodded.

"Maybe they didn't think they had the time to get his arm rebandaged and get back on our trail." No doubt

Beechner and Yorty had objected. They'd probably taken their fresh horses at gunpoint. I noticed they all had saddles and bridles and I doubted if any of them had possessed enough money to pay for them.

We avoided the Apache wickiups which lay along the broad valley and reached the agency buildings from the rear. No smoke rose from any chimney so we went on past, straight to the stable.

The first thing I saw when we rode up the inclined wooden ramp into the stable was the spread-eagled body of a man. I was off my horse instantly and knelt by his side. There was no movement in his chest. I picked up his right wrist and felt for pulse. There wasn't any.

There was a spot of blood in the center of his chest. He had been murdered in cold blood. A smoldering gunnysack they had used to muffle the sound of the shot lay nearby. I stamped out the sparks.

I looked at Lu's face. It was virtually expressionless, as if that was what she had expected to find here all along. I said, "Let's get some horses."

I mounted and we rode out of the stable again, circling the weather-beaten building to the corrals at the rear. The three Apache ponies Beechner, Yorty and Paddock had been riding weren't hard to pick out. All were lathered from hard traveling.

I selected two horses I thought would do, both bays so that they would be less noticeable from a distance, both by the Apaches and by the three men ahead of us. I started to lay the gunnysacks across my horse's back, then had second thoughts about keeping the money with me. If I hid the money here, nobody would know. The stableman was dead and nobody else was around. I climbed to the loft.

There was some hay up here, not much because the agency hayfields hadn't yet been cut. I'd have to find a place to hide the money where it wouldn't be found by the Indians storing the new crop up here.

There were half a dozen barrels of grain near the ladder I had climbed to get to the loft. Each had a cover to keep out the mice. I uncovered each one to see how full they were. Only one was full. Two were completely empty, two were partially full.

I dropped the gunnysacks into one of the empty ones. Then, straining, I lifted one that was half full and dumped it over them. I couldn't lift the full one, so I used a rusty bucket to transfer the oats from the full barrel to the one into which I had put the gunnysacks. The barrel holding the money was now the full one. There were still two partially filled barrels and two empty ones, just as before. I rearranged them so that they were positioned the same way as they had been, then got myself a handful of hay and used it like a broom to brush away marks where the barrels had been sitting and my own footprints. I climbed down the ladder. "The money is in the full grain barrel. It'll be safe there until we can get back."

She nodded disinterestedly. She didn't care any more than most Indians did about money. It was just paper to her, and metal shaped into round disks and stamped with various designs.

I knew I had to tell the agent about the stableman's murder. Maybe he could get a telegram off to Fort Chiricahua and have the three killers arrested when they arrived.

Walking toward the agent's quarters, leading the two horses, I thought that my job kept getting tougher all the time. I'd started out pursuing the killer of Mr. Satterfield.

Instead of catching him, I'd caught Paddock, who was a hell of a lot worse. Now I was pursuing three killers. But at least the money was safe, although I knew if I let myself be caught by the three instead of catching them, they'd get its location out of me quickly enough. If not by torturing me, then by torturing Lu. I'd tell about the money before I'd let them hurt her anymore.

The agent, a thin man of medium height, answered the door after my first knock. His face was deeply seamed, his blue eyes deeply sunken. I think his face might ordinarily have been a kind one, but now it was filled with worry and showed the effects of sleeplessness. His eyes were red. Almost irritably he asked, "Well, what is it? What is it now?"

I said, "I'm Jason Cole." He could see the deputy marshal's badge so I didn't have to identify myself further. I said, "I'm chasing three men, all of which are murderers. They killed your stableman."

"Luke? Oh, my God!" He pushed past us and ran toward the stable, with the two of us following. When we got there, he was already kneeling beside the body of the stableman. He turned his head and looked up. "You say white men did this? Are you sure it wasn't Apaches?"

I said, "I'm sure. The blood is still seeping from his wound. And we followed them here. They wanted saddles and fresh horses and he probably refused to give them up until he was paid for them." I then told him about making our way to the stage station and finding it besieged by Apaches. After I finished the story he seemed to believe me.

"Do you know where they went?"

I realized that I didn't know for sure. The three were after us, but when they discovered where our tracks left the road and led to here, their actions would become unpredictable. They might expect us to stay on the reservation where there would be safety with the agent and the agency Indians. Or they might expect me to be rash and head for Fort Chiricahua.

What I ought to do was retrieve the money from its hiding place and hotfoot it back to Alkali Flat with it. I tried to guess what Marshal McCabe would do if he was in my shoes. I knew immediately. He'd go after the three killers, placing secondary importance on the money.

The agent's name was Gaunt. I said, "Mr. Gaunt, maybe you can get a telegraph message off to the commandant at Fort Chiricahua to send troops to the stage station and to have him arrest those three when they arrive."

"How do you know they're going there?"

"It's a long story. I don't *know,* but I'm pretty sure. And a telegram sure can't hurt anything."

He nodded agreement. The lines seemed deeper in his face, his eyes more sunken and bloodshot than before. He said, "I don't know why I ever took this job. Half the Apache men are off the reservation and roaming the countryside, killing and burning. The rest are liable to go at any time. And I don't have any means of stopping them. Except words," he added wryly. "And they stopped listening to words a long time ago. They may even decide to come here and kill *me* before they leave."

I got the impression he wouldn't care too much if they did. I asked as we walked along the gallery toward the telegrapher's shack, "Do you have a family, sir?"

"My wife. I sent her to Tucson a month ago. My children are grown."

We reached the telegrapher's shack, which was by itself at the end of the gallery. Gaunt went in and I followed. Lu stayed outside, probably to keep watch for Apaches. Gaunt said, "I want you to get off a message to the commandant at Fort Chiricahua."

The telegrapher, a scrawny, bald man, shook his head. "Can't," he said. "Line's just been cut. I haven't even had time to report it."

There didn't seem to be much more to say. My priorities had changed again. The three murderers could wait. The Army had to be notified. I thanked the agent, and Lu and I went out and mounted our horses. I thought briefly about the money. Should I retrieve it and take it with me?

No, the money was safest right where it was. It was on the bottom of the full grain barrel, safe from mice. Furthermore, the partly empty grain barrels would be used before the full one was.

As before, we avoided the wickiups of the Apaches who were staying at the reservation. We struck the road at about the same place we had left it. We rode for several miles before I dismounted and studied the road for tracks. I found them and studied the patterns the hoofs made. Remounting we went on, both of us exceedingly watchful because neither of us knew but what the three would lay an ambush. They expected us to come this way.

Coming around a bend in the road, we ran unexpectedly into five Apache bucks. They were dressed exactly as Lu was, breechclout, high moccasins, cotton shirts issued to them by the Indian agent and some with faded-blue Army tunics, some with brass buttons and one with tarnished gold epaulets. All were painted and carried short-barreled, single-shot, trapdoor rifles, some .50

caliber buffalo guns that had been sawed off, some 45-70 Army pieces that had also been sawed off to make carbines out of them.

In all they had five shots without reloading. We had almost twenty. Lu wasn't used to using a revolver, and I didn't expect much help from her. But I raised my revolver and dropped the lead Apache off his horse, which immediately ran for the brush on the hillside. The others scattered, but I had time to kill one of their horses before they got out of range.

Immediately, I looked around for cover. There wasn't any, save for a clump of organ-pipe cactus. It must have had twenty stalks, some dead, some still living and covered with spines. There was cover enough for Lu and me behind the base of the cactus clump, but our horses would be exposed. I knew we had to get the Apaches' horses before the Apaches got us. I didn't even consider trying to kill the Apaches themselves. In the first place they presented smaller targets than their horses did. In the second place, I still didn't know for sure how Lu felt about Apaches, and I didn't want to risk alienating her by murdering Apache men when killing their horses would be just as effective.

I flopped down behind the cactus, paying no attention to where the horses went. I got a chance to kill a second Apache horse, and did so. All this time, Apache bullets were thudding into the organ-pipe cactus, and occasionally shreds of it dropped down on us.

Lu now had her revolver resting against one of the cactus stalks. With its barrel, she had stripped the spines from the stalk so that they would not hinder her. She fired, and a third horse went down.

This left the Apaches with only two horses. I waited,

expecting them to take the two horses and get the hell out of here.

But they didn't, and their painted faces told me why. They had committed themselves to war with the white man, and being such a small group were probably on their way to join a much larger and more effective group.

The trouble was, I didn't know exactly how far ahead of us Beechner, Yorty and Paddock were. They might be close enough to hear the shots, which would mean they'd hotfoot it back here and if the Apaches didn't get us, they would. I had to finish this and get off the road.

I whispered to Lu, "They've got single-shot rifles just like that other bunch did. I'm going to expose myself and draw their fire. As soon as all five have fired, I'm going to rush them. I'll try to kill their horses, but I may have to kill some of the men. Will that upset you?"

She shook her head. "They are trying to kill us. There is nothing wrong with defending ourselves."

I nodded, relieved. I didn't want to incur Lu's hatred by killing some of her tribesmen and possibly her relatives. I stuck my head up, holding my Spencer out in front of me, as if looking for a target. My revolver was already in its holster. I waited until I saw their heads raise up above the short clumps of sagebrush behind which they were concealed. I waited until I was looking straight down the bore of one of those old cannons they carried. Then I ducked.

Immediately, those old guns roared ahead of me. I counted the shots. One, two, three, four. I didn't hear the fifth.

The bastards were smarter than I'd given them credit for, I thought. One had held his fire, to cover the other four. But I was committed. If I didn't rush them now, we'd either be pinned down here until the gunfire brought Apache reinforcements, or until Beechner, Yorty and Paddock heard and returned.

I charged recklessly toward the Apaches, holding my Spencer carbine at the ready. When I got to within twenty-five feet, I killed their two remaining horses with three quick shots.

Four of the Apaches were busy reloading their guns. The fifth had his raised.

I knew I had to take time to aim carefully. The target was a lot smaller than a horse and I didn't dare miss. I stopped in my tracks, raised my gun, and fired.

A Spencer slug has considerable weight and mine hit him squarely in the breastbone. He was flung back as if he'd been kicked by a mule.

I couldn't worry about killing the Indians now. Their guns would have been reloaded. I fired four more times, as quickly as I could with accuracy. When the echoes of the gunfire had died away, five Apaches and four horses lay dead in front of me.

I jacked another cartridge into the Spencer and fumbled in my pockets for more. I walked to the Indians, stirring each with my foot to make sure they were dead. Then I turned and went back to where Lu still was. I said, "I'm sorry."

And now I discovered the difference in outlook between whites and Indians. Lu, practical and fatalistic, knew I'd had no choice. I even saw admiration in her eyes for the swift, unhesitating way I had done what had to be done. She knew we could have tried retreating. She also knew the Apaches would have followed us. It had been kill or be killed and she seemed to admire the swift dispatch with which I had disposed of the Indians.

Race no longer entered into her thinking. She had lived, had grown up with the Apaches. She had been married to a white. She had no reason to be grateful to either. Her father had traded her to Paddock as if she had been a horse or a goat. Paddock had mistreated her. As far as race was concerned, she was a free woman.

Except for me. I'd rescued her from Paddock. I had protected her. I faced a truth I had only skirted around before. She could not return either to Paddock or the Indians. And after all the Apaches she had killed or helped to kill, she would not be welcome in their wickiups.

She was alone or she was mine. And I wouldn't cut her adrift and leave her, no matter what.

CHAPTER 12

Our horses had not been touched by the Apache gunfire, but it had frightened them. They had trotted back two or three hundred yards into the cactus and brush. We caught them without much difficulty and, having done so, I knelt in the dusty roadway and again studied the tracks left there by Paddock, Yorty and Beechner.

In deep dust, it is always hard to tell how old a track is. They might be hours old; they might be minutes. If they were less than an hour old, it was practically certain Beechner, Yorty and Paddock would lay an ambush for us. If they'd heard the gunfire, dominated by that of the Spencers, they'd lay an ambush immediately.

We therefore had a couple of alternatives. We could head south, avoiding the road and the risk it presented from Apache war parties. Or we could go on to warn the fort, risking ambush by Paddock, Yorty and Beechner. This was the alternative I found more attractive. Lieutenant Wolcott and his men were white. Women were at the stagecoach depot, and their fate would be terrible if the depot was captured by the Indians.

I made my decision. I stopped long enough for Lu to catch up with me. I said, "Your husband and those other two are ahead of us. Their tracks were the only ones in the road and by now they know we are behind them."

She waited, the glance of her large, dark eyes resting

steadily on my face. I said, "If we are attacked, I want you to ride back to the agency. Wait there for Marshal McCabe and his posse. When he arrives, tell him where the money is and where I've gone. He'll bring the posse and come after us."

"By then you will be dead."

I shook my head. "I'm pretty damn hard to kill."

"It would be better if I stayed. I can help."

I looked at her, studying her face and eyes. I shook my head. "You might be killed. Or badly hurt. It won't make any difference to them whether they're shooting at a man or woman. And—" I hesitated for a moment and then said, "I don't think I could stand it if anything happened to you."

It was the closest I had come to letting Lu know how I had begun to feel about her. She lowered her glance so I wasn't able to see what her eyes revealed. I said, "Promise."

She raised her glance and firmly shook her head. Her eyes met mine steadily, holding an expression in some ways inscrutable, yet telling me something at the same time. There was warmth in her eyes but there was also a warning. I interpreted it to mean that she wasn't ready to commit herself either to me or to living again in the white man's world. Maybe it was my age. But I'd show her that age didn't matter. I'd show her I was mature enough to take care of her. If she wanted to stay with me that was all right. She might be safer anyway.

Right now I had sense enough *not* to ride along the road and into the ambush Paddock and the other two most certainly would have laid for us. I left the road immediately and headed west toward the telegraph line that ran between Fort Chiricahua and the Indian agency.

Maybe I could find where it had been cut and splice it. If I could succeed in doing that, the commandant at the fort would know about the uprising a long time before I could get there and tell him about it.

The line was no more than half a mile from the road, strung between twisted cedar poles, some of them no more than ten feet tall. Trees and brush had been cut along the right-of-way, so traveling beneath the line was easy for the horses.

No more than a dozen miles north of the agency, I found the place where the line had been cut. An Indian must have climbed one of the cedar poles and sawed the wires in two with a knife.

Immediately I saw that splicing the lines wasn't going to be easy. It would take all the strength I possessed to pull the line ends together. I wasn't sure I could get enough slack to make a splice.

I rode close to the pole where the short ends dangled. I stood up in the saddle and with my knife peeled the insulation from the wires. I got down and dismounted. I picked up the long ends and peeled them similarly. I looped them through the hondo on my lariat, rode back to the other pole and, standing in the saddle, tried to pull the ends together. By passing my rope around the pole I succeeded in pulling the wires close enough together to touch them, but try as I would, I could not get enough slack to make even the crudest kind of splice. If I'd had a foot of extra wire I could have managed it. Without extra wire, splicing was impossible.

I freed my rope and looked at Lu. "I'd kind of hoped I could tie those two ends together. Then we wouldn't have had to go to the fort." But even as I said it, I knew it wasn't strictly true. I would still have been committed to capturing Paddock and returning him for trial.

Following the telegraph line, we continued toward the fort. It occurred to me that maybe if we traveled half a dozen miles or so, then returned to the road, we might be able to slip up ahead of Paddock and the other two and lay an ambush for them while they were busy laying in ambush for us.

I suggested the plan to Lu. I could see the fear that showed in her eyes at the prospect of encountering Paddock again and I knew it would be unfair of me to force her into a situation she feared so much.

I said, "All right. Maybe it wasn't such a good idea. Let's get on to the fort."

I urged my horse to a lope and Lu kept pace. The miles fell behind. At about noon I stopped to let the lathered horses cool. Both Lu and I drank a little water from the single canteen we had. There was no food. Her wound seemed to be less painful and she was only slightly favoring the bandaged shoulder.

I had been wrestling with my feelings toward Lu all morning, and trying to decide in my mind what I would say to her. Thinking about what I would say didn't clarify anything, though, and I knew the best way was to just plunge in. I said, "I've mentioned this before, but the time's coming soon when we may not have a chance to talk about it. When we reach the fort, the commandant is going to separate us and I may not get a chance to say what I want to say."

She met my glance with her own, waited an instant and then said softly, "Maybe it would be better if we did not talk about it. You are very young and you have your whole life ahead of you. And you know how people in this territory feel about men who live with Indians." She avoided the word "squaw," for which I was grateful.

I opened my mouth to argue with her, but she spoke before I could. "Besides, you need time to consider your feelings. Right now you are sorry for me. You have not had much contact with women. In a year, or two, you will be sorry."

I said angrily, "And if you don't stay with me, what will you do? Paddock will either be dead or in prison. You can't go back to the reservation. What else is there?"

The question was unnecessary. I knew how few choices she was going to have.

I said firmly, "I'm not going to change. And I'm not going to let you get away from me. Unless you think I'm just a stupid kid and you've got something better in mind."

I knew by the expression in her eyes that what I'd suggested wasn't so. Her glance clung to me, and for the first time I saw tears in her eyes. I put my arms around her awkwardly and held her close against my chest. I said, "It's settled, then. When we leave the fort, you're going with me."

She drew away, avoiding meeting my glance directly. There was moisture on her cheeks but despite that, I had a distinctly uneasy feeling that nothing was really settled at all. My mind might be made up, and maybe hers was too, but I couldn't help feeling that we were still miles apart.

I decided, then, that I'd keep an eye on her. And before this was finished I'd convince her somehow that staying together was better for both of us.

We mounted and went on. The horses had cooled but

their neck hair was stiff with dried sweat. Again we held them to a lope whenever the terrain permitted.

I scowled to myself. Eighteen I might be, but I knew what I wanted. I wanted Lu. And I knew I wasn't going to change.

She, on the other hand, thought she would be a hindrance to me. She intended, I was sure, to disappear as soon as she knew that I was safe.

Knowing it was premature but also aware I would feel better if I could keep my eyes on her, I stopped. I said, "You go ahead."

Her expression was puzzled and questioning, but she moved on ahead without protest.

If I'd thought there was any chance of being ambushed as we rode along this telegraph right-of-way, I'd never have let her take the lead. But I felt sure Paddock and the other two were waiting for us on the road.

Besides, I enjoyed watching her, her straight back, her slender neck and the way she held her head.

She must have felt me watching her because she turned her head and looked at me. And I was surprised to see how bright were her eyes even though she tried to smile.

She had made up her mind all right. She was going to disappear as soon as she knew I was safe. But I was equally determined not to let her get away.

CHAPTER 13

We reached Fort Chiricahua in late afternoon. It looked like anything but a fort. The white frame buildings of the officers' quarters and headquarters were laid out on two sides of the square that formed the parade. On one of the other two sides were three barracks built of adobe bricks and roofed with heavy poles over which brush and earth had been thrown. It rained little in this part of the territory, so it wouldn't have taken much to keep the interior dry.

The fourth side of the square was made up of the stables, storehouses and corrals. A creek ran along this side and one corner of the corral was built so that it reached and crossed the creek. There was a hill beyond the creek on which a waist-high shelter for pickets had been built so they could see the creek bed, corrals and stables and give the alarm in case of an Indian raid.

We rode in on the near side, which happened to be between two of the barracks buildings. We were challenged almost immediately by a sentry whose voice was deep at first but broke halfway through the challenge. "Halt. Who goes there?"

A recruit, I thought, maybe standing his first sentry duty. I said, "Deputy Marshal Jason Cole, soldier. I want to see the commandant."

"Who's that with you?"

I saw him now, and he didn't look like he could be more than sixteen years old. He was towheaded, with the straw-colored hair sticking out beneath his blue forage cap. He held his rifle across his chest.

"This is Mrs. Paddock."

"How come she's wearing the get-up of an Apache buck?"

"That's too long a story for right here, soldier. Just pass us so we can see the commandant."

"Can't do that. But I'll call the corporal of the guard."

He did. "Corporal of the guard! Post number six!"

That word was passed along the line. After a few minutes I saw a stubby man wearing a corporal's stripes approaching us.

He appeared to be at least forty-five years old. His face was seamed and dark from exposure to the desert sun. His hair was graying and there was a vague, washed-out quality about his blue eyes that I had always associated with men who drank heavily. It probably explained why he was still a corporal at his age.

He asked, "What you want, youngster?"

"To see the commandant."

"That badge ain't yours, is it?"

"It is."

"What do you want to see the commandant about?"

"An Apache attack south of the San Carlos agency."

He peered at my face closely after that. "All right, bucko. You an' yer lady get down off them horses an' follow me. But Lord help you if you ain't tellin' the truth."

Lu and I dismounted and, leading our horses, followed the corporal. The sentry resumed his pacing but kept his face turned curiously toward us.

We reached the far side of the parade and the corporal

knocked on the door of a large building with a sign that designated it as headquarters. A voice told him to enter and he did. We followed. The corporal said, "This youngster with the badge claims he's a deputy marshal, Colonel. Says there's an Apache attack south of San Carlos."

The man behind the desk was tall and thin and wore a gray mustache and Vandyke beard. He said, "All right, Corporal."

The corporal plainly wanted to stay, but he had been dismissed. He saluted, turned abruptly and left. The colonel said, "I'm Colonel Hardesty."

I said, "I'm Jason Cole. From Alkali Flat. This here is Mrs. Paddock."

"What's this about an attack?"

I said, "It's at the stagecoach way station between the San Carlos agency and the Tucson road. I'd guess fifty Indians. Your paymaster and his escort are there. So are some miners and they've got a lot of gold. The stationmaster thinks the Indians are after the gold and the payroll as well as the guns. Otherwise, he says, they'd have taken what horses they could get and skedaddled a long time ago."

Colonel Hardesty studied my face carefully. I could tell he was wondering if I was telling the exact truth. It was dusk by now and he knew he couldn't do much of anything before dawn anyway. He said, "Tell me the whole story. How did you happen to be there? And who's this woman you've got with you? And why is she dressed in the clothes of an Apache buck?"

I sat down on a straight-backed chair and the colonel waved Lu to another one. I began telling him the story, starting with the shot I'd heard from the jail in Alkali Flat.

When I had finished, the colonel asked, "Where's the money now?"

I said, "Colonel, I don't see how I can tell you that."

His eyes narrowed slightly. "Surely you don't mistrust *me?*"

"No, sir. It's just that I know Paddock and those other two are going to try and pull the wool over your eyes. They'll say I'm not a deputy marshal. They're liable to say anything to make Lu look bad. And if you was to believe them instead of me, then I'd sure be mighty sorry I told you where the money was. I'll get it myself when all this has quieted down. I'll turn it over to Marshal McCabe. He can return what was taken from Satterfield's and maybe he can find out who the rest belongs to once he's dug up them bodies and tried to put names to them."

"How many bodies?"

"Seven. Counting the one I was chasing."

The colonel nodded, frowning. "It's hard to believe."

There was a knock on the door. The colonel called, "Come in," and a uniformed man entered, wearing a captain's bars on his shoulder. He looked at me, not missing the deputy marshal's badge, and then glanced at Lu. Despite her men's clothing, she was a damned attractive woman, and the captain's eyes showed his appreciation. The colonel said, "Captain Dennison, this is Jason Cole, who says he is a deputy U.S. marshal, and Mrs. Paddock, who he claims to have rescued from a severe beating at the hands of her husband."

The way he put it, it sounded like everything I'd told him was a pack of lies. I began to wonder what would happen when Paddock and the two drifters showed up. The colonel would probably take their word against mine. I began to wish I'd never come.

Captain Dennison asked, "Mind repeating your story for me, young man?"

I did, starting in Alkali Flat and ending here. He asked, "What'd you do with the money? If you had it, it would make your story a lot easier to believe."

The colonel said, "I asked him the same question. He says he won't tell anybody but Marshal McCabe where he's hidden it."

Dennison said, "Jim, we don't dare disbelieve him. We've known for a long time that the Apaches didn't want to stay at San Carlos."

"What if Paddock and the two with him tell a different story?"

Dennison shrugged. "Let's get ready on the strength of this boy's story. Give me two troops. I'll have them ready to go by sunup. If those other three arrive with a different story, then we can decide which story we'd rather believe. But at least we'll be ready."

The colonel studied my face. I could feel myself getting angrier all the time. They looked at me as if I was a bug mounted on a cork with a pin and they talked about me as if I was a fifteen-year-old boy.

Finally the colonel nodded grudgingly. "Take troops B and F. You'll need rations for a week, and take the surgeon and an ambulance. There may be some casualties at that way station."

The captain saluted casually and left. Colonel Hardesty looked at me. "You can sleep in the enlisted men's quarters, son. She"—he inclined his head toward Lu—"can go to the laundresses' quarters."

I could feel my anger increasing but I knew saying anything would not only be useless, it would probably make matters worse.

I went out, with Lu following. We headed out across the parade and as soon as we were out of hearing, Lu asked, "Where's the laundresses' quarters?"

"Damned if I know. Anyhow, you're not going to spend the night there. You know how they'd treat you if you did. Besides that, I'm getting damn tired of being called a boy."

Our horses were still tied in front of headquarters. I said, "Wait right here. I'll get our horses and we'll spend the night out in the brush someplace."

She stopped. I returned to headquarters, moving on silent feet. I untied the two horses. I led them back to where Lu was waiting.

Now I headed for the stables. Nobody was likely to question our movements as long as we were headed that way. Only we wouldn't stop at the corrals. We'd keep on going, most likely without even being seen.

We reached the stables and went beyond, to the corrals. Behind us I heard some shouting, which I supposed came from a sergeant to whom Captain Dennison had passed the word to ready two troops for moving out in the morning.

We went far enough away from the fort so that any Apaches watching it would be between us and the fort. Lu sat down with her back to a rock. There was a scrubby cedar nearby and I put my back to that. The altitude was higher here and the vegetation different. Also, it got cold during the night. It was already chilly and I knew it would get worse.

We had no blankets and Lu's clothes were in one of the gunnysacks along with the money. Lu said, "I'm glad you hid the money. If you hadn't, that colonel would have taken it away from you."

"So am I." There didn't seem to be much to say. Time wore on, stretching out from minutes to an hour or more, with neither of us saying anything. I was shivering myself and I suddenly became aware that Lu was too. I got up and moved over beside her. I sat down close and put my arm around her. I said lamely, "We can keep each other warm."

I'd tied the horses to the branches of the cedar, and I could hear them moving around, trying to reach grass clumps that seemed to be just out of their reach.

There was another long silence. Her body was warm against mine and both of us had stopped shivering. She laid her head against my shoulder as if it was the most natural thing in the world to do.

I wanted her, but I was young enough and dumb enough to want some kind of solid commitment at the same time. An older man would probably have made love to her without thinking twice.

Instead I said, "What about when this is all over? Have you really decided what you're going to do?"

Before she could answer I heard some shouting down at the fort. They must have discovered that we were gone, I thought. But the colonel hadn't talked to Paddock and the two with him because they hadn't yet arrived.

Lu said softly, "I don't know what I'm going to do."

Well, I'd made up my mind for sure by now. I said, "I want you to come with me. You're promised to me. Maybe we can't get married right away, at least until Paddock gets hung, but I can work and I can take care of you."

She was silent for a long time. When she did speak, her voice was hardly audible. "All right, Jason. I'll keep my promise. I will go with you."

It surprised me so that I didn't have anything to say. I just tightened my arm around her.

I couldn't help thinking, now, about Alkali Flat, where I'd spent my whole life so far. I thought about Sue Ann Satterfield, but I didn't think about her very long. When I compared her with Lu, she didn't come off looking very good. She was pretty all right, but she was soft and spoiled and she didn't have much use for me anyhow being as how I didn't belong to one of the town's better families. I didn't belong to any family at all and she'd never have married me if I'd courted her for thirty years.

And she could never have gone through what Lu had gone through.

Marshal McCabe. I could imagine the look on his face when I told him I was going away with Lu. It would get red and the veins would stand out on his forehead and then he'd yell at me. He'd tell me what a damn fool I was taking up with an Apache girl—and one who had been married to a killer to boot. He'd tell me he'd been going to get me appointed deputy U.S. marshal as soon as I was twenty-one years old. He'd say now that was out of the question. Nobody was going to appoint a squaw man deputy marshal or anything else. Then when I told him I was going to marry Lu white-man fashion as soon as Paddock was hanged, he'd just throw up his hands in disgust. Of course, he wouldn't do any of this in front of Lu. He wasn't much of a hand to cotton up to Apaches but he wasn't cruel and he knew they had feelings just like anybody else.

Lu said softly, "You're already sorry you asked me to go with you, aren't you?"

I turned and put both my arms around her. Her words

had made all my doubts disappear. I said, "No I'm not. I never will be."

"Then why were you so quiet?"

I grinned in the darkness. "Just thinking about the things Marshal McCabe is going to say."

"He will not approve?" She made it sound like a question, but it wasn't.

"No. He won't approve. Probably hardly anybody will, Apaches or white people. But I'm a man grown and I know what I want. I love you and I want you and I'll take care of you and be good to you. I can drive stage, or a freight wagon. There's lots of things that I can do."

"Jason . . ." There was suddenly doubt in her voice.

I took her face between my hands. I was close enough to see her face, on which the bruises hardly showed anymore. I said, "You promised me. And I've got to know that I can count on you."

There was a moment when fear was like something cold inside my chest. Then she nodded firmly. "You can count on me."

Right then I wanted her more than I had ever wanted anything. But I knew if anything happened between us out here tonight, Paddock would know it the minute he glimpsed my face and hers tomorrow morning. And if he made the colonel believe, then I'd be completely discredited.

CHAPTER 14

I awoke at dawn when gray first streaked the horizon. I was no longer leaning against the rock but was stretched out flat. Lu was pressed up close beside me. An early-morning chill was in the air, telling me the altitude here was greater than it was in Alkali Flat.

I stirred, and Lu awoke silently. Her eyes were large and dark and, coming out of a deep sleep, as soft as those of a doe.

A bugle blew reveille down at the fort, and after that there were a lot of men's voices shouting and the sounds of movement in the stables and horse corrals. Our own horses were still tied to the cedar, standing with heads hanging, half asleep themselves.

I smiled at Lu. I wanted to kiss her, but I didn't, maybe because her glance was resting so steadily on me. I'd have to get over that, I thought with self-disgust. That was a kid's reaction and starting now I was going to have to stop being a kid and be a man.

I got to my feet. "We'd just as well go on down. Your husband and those other two will be there by now." I had to grin a little, thinking what their reactions were going to be when they found out we neither had the gunnysacks nor had turned them in to the post commandant.

We untied our horses and mounted. I led the way and we picked our way down to the stable area. Soldiers were busy everywhere, catching their horses, checking shoes, carefully saddling so that no wrinkle in the saddle blanket would later make the horse unserviceable. I figured I'd just as well get the confrontation with Paddock and his two companions over with, so I left Lu with the surgeon to have her shoulder dressed and walked toward the headquarters building. I had withdrawn my Spencer from the saddle boot and I had my revolver belted around my waist. I didn't think any one of the three would attack me without first knowing where the money was but I was taking no chances.

I saw Beechner first. He was on foot, leading his horse toward the stables. Yorty followed him, and Paddock brought up the rear. Paddock was showing the strain of his broken arm now. Despite the fact that it had been splinted and placed in a sling, it still must cause him considerable pain because his face was almost gray and his lips were thinned, pressed together to conceal the pain. His eyes were hollow, and beneath them the skin was dark.

When he saw me, his eyes changed. They blazed with fury and with hate. If he'd had the use of both hands I don't doubt for a minute that he'd have tried to shoot me. The trouble was, one hand was in a sling and his horse's reins were in the other.

All three men stopped. Paddock said savagely, "You son-of-a-bitch! Where is she? And where are those gunnysacks?"

I swung my Spencer around so that it loosely covered the three of them. I said, "The money's in a safe place. Mrs. Paddock is back there at the surgeon's getting a bullet wound dressed."

Paddock said, "You boys take him. If we can get him

off this damned Army post a mile or two he'll damn soon tell us where the money is."

I jacked a cartridge into the Spencer. I said, "Sure, boys. Take me."

Both Beechner and Yorty were also scowling now. I thought Paddock was going to have a stroke. His face was beet-red and the veins on his forehead stood out, throbbing.

Beyond the three, I saw Captain Dennison step out of the colonel's headquarters office. He strode rapidly toward us. He looked from the faces of Paddock, Beechner and Yorty to mine. He switched his glance back from my face to those of the other three. He said harshly, "All of you are going to have to forget your quarrel. This command is moving out in thirty minutes and you all will accompany it." His glance didn't return to me and I had the feeling he would a lot rather believe me than Paddock, Beechner and Yorty. I turned and headed back toward the stables. The other three didn't stir for a moment and Dennison barked, "Move, damn you!"

Sullenly they headed toward the stables, following me, staying about fifty feet behind. Dennison glared at them a moment, then I turned my head and couldn't see him anymore. I knew not one of the three was a threat to my life at least as long as they didn't know where the money was.

I reached the stables. The corrals lay beyond. I didn't see Lu anywhere, although I saw our two horses. They were eating hay from a pile on the ground. The horses belonging to the cavalry were either in the corrals or were being led toward the stables by sleepy-looking troopers.

It wasn't like Lu to just leave the horses and it puzzled me. I called, "Lu?"

There was a bustle of noise all around me, but over it all I thought I heard a small cry from the stable loft directly overhead.

Paddock, Beechner and Yorty had arrived by now and they were looking at our horses even though it was plain enough that neither horse carried anything.

I called, "Lu?" again, but this time there was no reply.

I was suddenly overcome with concern. Lu had probably climbed into the loft so that she could throw hay down to our horses. But something had happened to her—maybe she'd caught her foot in something—hell, I didn't know. All I knew was that I'd heard a small and quickly stifled cry.

I whirled and entered the wide double doors of the stable. There was a ladder about halfway back, barely visible in the early light. I ran toward it and climbed it as rapidly as I could.

My head came level with the floor of the loft. I saw something: some movement toward the front part of the loft. I heard the crackling of hay.

I finished climbing to the level of the loft floor and ran toward the movement I had seen.

Halfway there, I knew what it was. Two struggling figures, one of which had to be Lu. It was her voice that had cried out, probably muffled by a man's heavy hand over her mouth.

The raw fury that overcame me surprised me. I suddenly wanted to kill this man who had seized Lu and was trying to violate her. Running, I covered the distance separating us in a split second. I was ten feet away before I could distinguish Lu from the man in the very dim light.

My Spencer was leaning against the wall at the foot of

the ladder where I'd left it when I started to climb. It's probably a good thing it was, because I might have killed the man if I'd had a gun in my hand.

I aimed a kick at his head, heard it connect solidly, and suddenly he lost all interest in Lu. He released her and she scrambled away, got to her feet and began to rearrange her clothes.

The man was stunned, but he knew he had been caught and he apparently had recognized me. He got to his feet, weaving, his belt unfastened and his pants unbuttoned. I stepped in close and landed a fist squarely on his nose.

It burst like a ripe tomato, splattering blood in every direction. He took a couple of steps backward. His pants fell down, tripping him, and he sprawled flat on his back in the hay.

My kick and the blow to his nose had him pretty groggy. I grabbed one of his heavy Army shoes and dragged him toward the loft door. When I got him there, I put a toe under his body and rolled him out. He fell, lit on his back in such a way that all the wind was knocked out of him. Afterward he lay there, pants down to his knees, dirty Army-issue underwear showing below his shirttail.

My anger wasn't satisfied, but there wasn't much more I could do to the man right now. Lu was already going down the ladder and I followed her in time to retrieve my Spencer at the foot of it. She put a hand on my arm and said, "No. The Army will take care of him."

And the Army, in the person of Captain Dennison, had already begun to take care of the matter by the time we reached the front doors of the stable. He was standing there, face red with fury, staring down at the man trying to get his breath on the ground, not even yet aware that his pants were down around his ankles.

The captain glanced at Lu, then at me, then roared, "Sergeant!"

A sergeant approached at a trot. Dennison said icily, "Throw this man in the stockade. I'll take care of him when we get back."

"The colonel will want to know the charge, Captain."

"Attempted rape. Now get him out of here!"

The sergeant stirred the man on the ground with the toe of his heavy boot in what was more a kick than anything gentler. The man got up awkwardly, trying to pull up his pants as he did.

He moved away, with the sergeant close behind. But before he left he grumbled at Lu, "Only a lousy Indian squaw!" Then he was gone.

Dennison turned to Paddock, Beechner and Yorty. "When did you three arrive?"

"Last night. Midnight, maybe."

"Then you haven't talked to the colonel?"

"No, sir." That was Beechner.

"All right. Let me hear your story then."

"Long story, Captain. Why don't we tell it to you while we ride?"

Dennison shrugged. I knew damned well why Beechner didn't want to tell him their story now. They hadn't yet gotten together and decided what it was going to be. And since it was all going to be lies, they didn't want to get caught in any.

Lu and I stood beside our horses and let them eat until we heard the bugle blow assembly. Her arm had been neatly bandaged. Then we led them down to the creek and let them drink. I found a gunnysack with no holes in it and filled it about a quarter full of oats, thinking as I did about the money hidden underneath the grain at the Indian agency.

Paddock, Beechner and Yorty were ready, having been given fresh horses. They were by themselves in one corner of the parade, talking earnestly. The two troops formed on the parade amid the shouts of their sergeants and corporals. The lines straightened in spite of the eager, nervous prancing of the cavalry mounts.

I watched the captain, sitting his horse in front of headquarters talking to the colonel. Something had struck me as familiar about him last night and again this morning and suddenly I knew what it was. He reminded me of Marshal McCabe.

Finally the captain shouted an order, one which was repeated over and over down the line of mounted men.

At the order to execute, the line of men turned, forming a column of twos. They left by the gate between headquarters building and the one next to it. There was a wooden arch over the gate, with cut-out wooden letters forming the words "Fort Chiricahua."

Lu and I climbed into our saddles and I kicked my horse in the ribs and rode to the head of the column to join Captain Dennison. Lu followed me.

Dennison looked at me. I said, "They're cooking up their story. When they've got it ready, they'll come and lay it out for you."

He nodded, whether in agreement or not I couldn't tell. He was busy looking back at the column as it followed out through the gate. The ambulance was between the two troops, the surgeon sitting beside the driver.

Dust rose in a blinding cloud. A breeze cleared it away

long enough for me to see a cluster of women standing near the colonel in front of headquarters.

And then the last of the second troop cleared the gate and we were on the road leading south past the San Carlos agency to the way station that was under attack.

Unless the way station had already been overwhelmed. And that was possible.

CHAPTER 15

The road between Fort Chiricahua and the San Carlos Indian agency is fairly well defined, not so much as a result of wheeled vehicles traveling it as by horseback travel, and it is therefore wider than it otherwise would be. Furthermore, there are many shortcuts, easy for horses but difficult for the wagons, ambulances and stagecoaches, which generally stick to the two-track wagon road.

Captain Dennison, despite his apparent youth (I judged him to be under forty), seemed to be an experienced campaigner. He led his troops at a steady trot, knowing it to be one of the easiest gaits for horses and further knowing there would be no replacements along the way for horses that got worn out.

Actually, Captain Dennison only seemed young to me by comparison with the colonel, who was considerably older. When you're eighteen, everybody over thirty seems old and some do who are under that.

Dennison rode at the head of the column, along with the civilian scout, a gray-bearded oldster in greasy, rancid buckskins named Swope. If he had a Christian name, I never heard it.

Lu and I rode behind, and behind us was a second lieutenant named McPheeters, in command of F Troop. I knew that ordinarily a captain commanded a troop, but since the war, funding had been cut drastically for the

Army on the frontier, particularly since it wasn't a frontier anymore and it was generally thought the Apaches were safely confined to their reservations. Promotions came hard. McPheeters was fresh out of the academy and Dennison had been a major during the war. Afterward, his former lieutenant's rank had been restored and he'd only had one promotion since 1865.

We hadn't traveled more than a dozen miles before Paddock, Beechner and Yorty came galloping to the column's head. They crowded in between Lu and me and Captain Dennison and his scout. Paddock said, "Captain, sir, you got a few minutes to hear the true story about what happened between us and this kid?"

Dennison looked at him sternly. "If it's the *true* story, I have."

"Oh, it will be, sir, I can promise you." Paddock, for a surly, cold-blooded killer, was as ingratiating as a beggar.

Paddock said, "Well, he come ridin' down into my ranch a week or so ago. He come bustin' in. Lu an' me was only havin' an argument. Them bruises she got a couple days before when her horse throwed her in a pile of rocks. Pitiful sight it was. I fixed her up the best I could. And I wanted her to go see a doctor in Tucson. She wouldn't go, sir, and that was what the argument was about. This youngster butted in, and the vicious little bastard took advantage of me because I wouldn't use my gun and broke my arm. After that, it was pretty much all his way. He made Lu tell him where we kept what little money and valuables we had and he took it and put it in a gunnysack. Then he claimed I'd killed the man he was chasin', and tied me up. He forced both Lu and me to go with him until we got to that way station, where the stationmaster turned me loose."

Captain Dennison turned his head and looked at Lu. I knew he wasn't going to believe what she said over Paddock's word. He was just going through the motions. He asked, "Is that right, ma'am?"

She shook her head. "Not a word of it."

Dennison frowned. He wasn't a judge, just a captain of cavalry, and he wasn't supposed to have to make decisions like this. He said, "All right. What about these other two?"

Paddock said, "They'll have to speak for theirselves, sir."

I thought that was smart of him. If he'd spoken for Beechner and Yorty it would have been pretty obvious that the three of them had gotten together to cook a story up.

Dennison looked at Beechner. "Well?"

"Well, sir, we're messengers for a bank in Mesilla. We was carrying a shipment of gold to the Tucson bank."

"How much?"

"We didn't know, Captain. It was in a canvas bag with a lock on it. We was supposed to change it for paper money and bring it back."

"And this youngster got the gold?"

"No, sir. It wasn't gold. It was paper money from the Tucson bank. He happened on us, and when he seen we had money, he put a gun on us and took it away. He slashed open that locked bag and took the money out and put it in his gunnysacks."

Captain Dennison said drily. "Seems to me for an eighteen-year-old kid he didn't have a hell of a lot of trouble overpowering three grown men and taking the woman belonging to one of them. Where are these gunnysacks now?"

"He must've hid 'em, Captain, sir. But all we got to do is make him tell us where they are."

"How would you propose to do that?"

Paddock made his first mistake. "Just let us have him for about ten minutes, sir. He'll be glad to tell."

"You mean torture him?"

"He's a lousy little killer, sir."

Dennison looked weary of the whole conversation and his expression said he didn't believe a word of it. I started to open my mouth to ask the captain how come Beechner and Yorty had been so far north of the stage road that ran between Mesilla and Tucson and also why, when El Paso was so much closer, they hadn't been sent there to change their gold into paper money, but I didn't have to. Captain Dennison had already thought of it.

He asked, "That stagecoach way station is miles north of the road between Tucson and Mesilla. How'd you two happen to be that far off your course?"

That appeared to be a point the two hadn't considered. Both flushed slightly and finally Beechner said lamely. "'Paches chased us there, Captain, sir. I guess we could've gone back into the hills, but we figgered there'd sure enough be a stagecoach way station or something along that road where we could get shelter from them Indians."

Dennison was silent a moment. Finally he asked, "And was Mr. Paddock and this 'kid' with you all this time? Or did you encounter them after you got to the stagecoach depot?"

Yorty blurted, "They was with us. That kid had already robbed us of the money we was carryin'."

Simultaneously Beechner said, "No, sir. We didn't—" He stopped, realizing what Yorty was saying.

The captain said softly, "Get to the rear of the column, gentlemen. I am required to treat you with courtesy, but you make it hard. And if you give me any trouble after we get into action with the Indians—well, no more courtesy. Is that clear?"

Beechner opened his mouth to protest, but when Paddock nudged him, he shut his mouth and pulled out of the column with a murderous glance at me that included Lu. The three rode their horses toward the end of the column.

Captain Dennison glanced at me, anger still showing in his face. "Are you really a deputy U.S. marshal, son?"

The "son" irritated me, but I knew he meant it in a friendly way. I said truthfully, "No. But I help Marshal McCabe and I happened to be the only one in town who could do anything when Mr. Satterfield got killed."

Dennison said, "How old *are* you?"

I lied by a few months. "Eighteen, sir."

Dennison said, "I went through the war, son, and I know that age don't make a man. I've seen kids sixteen that were better men than a lot of 'em thirty-five and forty."

I said, "I'm trying, sir. Growing up takes time."

He glanced at Lu, and then, as if he'd forgotten she spoke perfect English, asked, "What about her?"

"She can't go back to the reservation. Her pa sold her to Paddock for some horses."

"She can't live in a white man's town."

I said, "Oh, yes, sir, she can. Paddock's going to get hung. Me and Lu are going to stay together."

"You'll never make U.S. marshal with an Apache wife."

I shrugged. "There's all kinds of jobs. And I'm handy."

He seemed to lose interest in the subject. He turned his

head and spoke in a low voice with the scout. I couldn't hear what he said, or what Swope replied. The breeze blew toward me from the scout and I thought that he smelled worse than any Apache I'd ever encountered. If the wind was right, I'd have bet an Apache could smell him fifty yards away.

But I wasn't really thinking of Swope, or the captain, or even of the Apaches. I was thinking about Paddock, Beechner and Yorty. They all had guns now, guns they'd either bought or stolen at the agency or at the fort.

Their having guns didn't worry me. Not exactly. They weren't going to kill me or even shoot me until they knew where I'd hidden the gunnysacks.

But they didn't need Lu, and by threatening her they could make me do anything they wanted me to. If they were able to get their hands on her.

We halted at noon, just short of the turnoff that led to the San Carlos Indian agency. Captain Dennison gave orders that the horses were to be watered and fed oats from the canvas morrals that each man carried on his saddle.

He then selected the scout and half a dozen men to accompany him to the agency to see if any assistance was needed there. It occurred to me that he might requisition some grain for his horses and I didn't want anybody messing around with those grain barrels unless I was present. I asked, "Captain, can Lu and me go with you?"

"Why?"

I looked toward the rear of the column. "To tell you the truth, sir, I'm kind of leery of Paddock and the two with him. They've all got guns now. And they know if they can get hold of Lu, I'll do anything they ask. We'd just feel safer if we was along with you."

"All right. Come on."

He rode away, followed by Swope, then by Lu and me. The six troopers brought up the rear.

I didn't think there was any danger for this small a group riding through the wickiups of the reservation Apaches. Those that were still here on the reservation were peaceable. The malcontents and hostiles had already left.

We trotted along the road until the Apache wickiups came into view. Women and children and a few old men came out to stare at us. I didn't see a single man between the ages of sixteen and forty.

I looked at Lu. The only signs now visible of the beating Paddock had given her were a few greenish spots on her face where the bruises had been. I said, "Paddock knows how you and me feel about each other. So he'll try to get you away. He knows that all he has to do is threaten you and I'll tell him where the money is. So stay close to me. And keep your gun handy. Shoot all three if they get too close."

After I'd said it, I knew my advice wasn't very good. If she should shoot one of the three, she'd be brought into court and tried for her crime just like any other killer because it would be impossible for her to prove that she had acted in self-defense.

The only other solution was for me to stay close to her.

I'd sworn to myself that I'd bring the money back, and that I'd bring Paddock back to hang for the murders he had committed. But away down deep I knew that if Lu was threatened with imminent torture and death, I'd let both Paddock and the money go.

I considered the possibility that my feelings for Lu might be a simple youthful crush. Then I turned my head and looked at her. Her mouth was full and soft, and her eyes revealed nothing of the years she had spent being brutalized by Paddock. Yet her chin was firm, showing the strength that had enabled her to come through those years relatively untouched.

We reached the agency compound and Captain Denison went inside to talk with the agent. The troopers dismounted and lounged in the shade, smoking and waiting.

To Lu I whispered, "I'll be back in a minute."

I left my horse and eased around a corner of the building. Once out of the sight of the troopers, I ran for the stable as fast as I could. On the way I spotted what must have been the new stableman hurrying toward the agent's office to find out what was going on. He must have seen the captain and his escort ride in.

That was a great relief to me. I reached the stable, went in and rapidly climbed the ladder to the loft.

The grain barrels were exactly as I had left them. I had made an indentation with my hand in the full one where the money was. The indentation was still there, still the same.

Aware of how dangerous it would be for me to be caught here, I went down the ladder. I stopped in the wide double doors to see if anyone was watching. Then I ran, by the same route I had come, back to the agent's office where Lu and the troopers still waited.

Lu's glance was questioning. I nodded slightly to let her know the grain barrel had not been touched.

The captain came out, accompanied by the agent. They talked a few minutes, then the captain stepped off the gallery and mounted his horse. With Swope at his side, he led out along the dusty road toward the place he had left his two troops.

When we arrived, Paddock, Beechner and Yorty had

disappeared. I worried briefly about whether they might not have followed us and seen me climb to the stable loft.

But I knew there was no use worrying. If they had, they would find the money and we would never see them again. I had been a fool to check the grain barrels, because checking them had served no purpose but to reassure me.

At least I still had Lu. And there was no reason for me to believe Paddock and his friends had seen me climb to the stable loft.

The captain gave the order to mount, and it was passed down the line by troop commanders and sergeants. We headed south again toward the stagecoach depot.

A couple of miles from the place we'd stopped, Paddock, Beechner and Yorty rejoined the column, appearing unobtrusively from a thick grove of cedars and head-high sagebrush.

I felt the relief run through me. If they'd found the money, they would not have returned to the column at all. It was still safe—in the grain barrel where I had stored it so carefully.

That worry was over with. But I knew they still were a deadly threat. They'd try to get Lu, or both of us, away from the column. Then, with practically no trouble at all, they'd get the location of the money out of us.

I knew that what I felt for her was no youthful infatuation. It was real and strong and lasting. She had become the most important thing in my life.

CHAPTER 16

I'd told him the telegraph lines were cut, so Dennison dispatched two men to the agency shops with instructions to get climbers, pliers and extra wire, and to repair it. They were also told to have the telegrapher check the lines leading south to make sure they had not also been cut. If they were, they were to ride beneath them until they located the break.

Having returned to the main command, we continued our journey south.

I dropped back slightly and drew my horse closer to Lu's. "Your husband and his two friends are going to try and get us away from the column. They have to. It's their only way out."

She nodded, and simultaneously both of us looked toward the end of the column where Paddock, Yorty and Beechner were. At the moment we couldn't see them because the column was going around a curve in the road and they were hidden behind a rocky ridge.

Or they were gone. It was possible they had left the column, veered off to one side, and were even now keeping pace, watching for an opportunity. I didn't dare to even let Lu leave the column to care for her private needs unless I went along as guard. Nor were my own chances much better if I got off by myself. Neither of the three would hesitate a minute about shooting the legs out from under me because they'd know that no matter how bad the wounds I'd live to tell them where the money was.

One thing I did know. I had to find out what they were up to, and when they intended to put their plan into effect. I said, "Stay right here, close to the captain. I'll be back in ten minutes. I want to ride to the end of the column and see if your husband and his friends are still with us."

"I wish you'd stop calling him my husband. It may be true legally but I'll never go back to him."

There was suddenly a flurry of shots from the steep hillside on our right. A trooper fell, blood streaming from his thigh, and his horse went running crazily down the road, blood soaking his side and belly from the jagged wound the misshapen bullet had gouged in his side after it exited from the trooper's leg.

Captain Dennison's reaction was instantaneous. He bawled, "Horse holders!" and "Take cover. No shooting unless you can see what you're shooting at."

I was two thirds of the way back along the column. But already I could see the end of it. Paddock, Beechner and Yorty were gone.

It was them, then, firing from the hillside, trying to make the captain believe he had been attacked by hostile Indians. More shots cracked from the hillside and a trooper's horse went down. I knew Paddock had no respect for human life and would have shot to kill. But Beechner and Yorty probably felt differently. They weren't above killing, but they wouldn't kill uselessly.

Apparently they had hidden themselves very well because their firing was not answered by the troops. Another trooper fell over backward, a stream of blood gushing from his throat. This one was dead before he hit the ground.

Suddenly I was mad. Two troopers had been wounded and another killed for the sole reason of drawing me away from the column or at least trying to separate me from it during the confusion of the attack.

All right. I'd leave the column. I'd take the battle to Paddock and his friends. If I could get behind them . . .

I left my horse and sprinted for the cover of a huge rock. Two troopers were also behind it, and they moved over to make room for me.

I waited until I heard Paddock, Beechner and Yorty firing again. Then I left the rock and sprinted back along the road, staying as close to the rocks as possible. I heard one of the troopers say contemptuously, "The yellow son-of-a-bitch! Look at him run! Leavin' his woman, too!"

It was a natural assumption, I guess, but it stung all the same. When I figured the men on the hillside couldn't see me anymore, if indeed they ever had after I'd left my horse, I turned and began to scramble up the hill. I had to be above them, I knew, before I would stand a chance against them. They were three and I was only one.

I climbed nearly to the top of the ridge, and then I had to stop. My clothes were soaked with sweat. It streamed off my forehead and into my eyes. I was breathing raggedly and it seemed as if each breath was hotter than the last.

I could still hear occasional rifle shots, both on the hillside and down on the road. Either the troopers had seen the men they were shooting at or they thought they had.

I climbed until I was bathed with sweat and until I thought I was going to faint from the heat. I was above them now, I thought. It was time to rest a moment, then parallel the hill until I was in a position to either kill or capture them. The captain would give me no trouble when I showed him that the attack on his column had been made by the three renegade whites.

I could still hear the gunshots, those from Paddock and his friends as well as those from the troopers on the valley floor. But I also heard shots midway up the hill between the cavalry column and the three renegades and I guessed that Captain Dennison had sent men up the hill to kill those who were shooting at him, which I am sure he supposed were Indians.

I was directly above Paddock, Beechner and Yorty now. Or at least I thought I was. Carefully, and as silently as I could, which was pretty quietly, I eased along the hill toward them. At any moment now I'd spot them and be able to aim my gun at them. They'd capitulate and if I wasn't killed by the infiltrating troopers, I'd be able to herd them on down the hill. I was pretty sure that the captain would put them in irons, which would mean no danger from them for the rest of the trip.

Suddenly, as I picked my way through a particularly thick clump of cactus, I heard Paddock's unmistakable, triumphant voice, "All right you stinkin' little son-of-a-bitch. Throw your guns down. You took the bait like a ten-year-old. Now we're going to find out where that money's hid."

Maybe I'd have tried escaping from Paddock, but at that instant I saw Yorty directly ahead of me, bellied down behind a thick clump of cholla cactus, his rifle aimed directly at me.

Well, I thought, I am still a goddamn kid. A man wouldn't have let them lure him away from the cavalry column like this.

Beechner appeared, his horse lunging up the steep hillside. The shooting stopped.

Bleakly I thought that the troopers Dennison had sent up the hillside would return when they found nobody within rifle range. And Paddock had what he wanted. He had me and it was a cinch he was going to enjoy the things he intended doing to me to unseal my lips.

Beechner got his horse, mounted and jabbed me with his rifle barrel. Paddock led the way, his unshaven, dirty face still twisted with the pain from his broken arm.

They went up over the hill with me stumbling along on foot. Yorty paused long enough to pick up my weapons and then he mounted and came too.

I don't know when my prospects have been so bleak. They had me and even if Captain Dennison knew it, his job wasn't to chase all over the countryside looking for me. It was to get to the stagecoach depot with all possible haste and rescue not only his paymaster and escort and the money they were carrying, but to rescue the other whites who were under siege.

So I could expect no help from Dennison. Most likely they were already riding south again. And I was unarmed, with no horse, held captive by three vicious and desperate men. They'd take me back away from the road half a mile or so, then torture me until I told them where the money was. After that, Paddock would kill me, in the most dragged-out, painful way he could devise. That prospect was terrifying.

We went down a long, shallow slope at the bottom of which was a bare area maybe fifty feet square, dotted with rocks and scrub cactus of the prickly pear variety.

Paddock halted his horse, turning his head to look at me. I hope that, as long as I live, I never see a look like that in another human being's eyes. To describe it accurately would be futile, because in it were combined so many things, all of them completely evil, and I knew my dying sure wasn't going to be quick. I doubted, furthermore, if either Beechner or Yorty would ever leave this small clearing alive.

Paddock, with one arm in the sling, couldn't handle a rope so he said shortly, "Yorty, put a rope on him."

Well, hell, I wasn't going to stand still for them. I turned and sprinted away, but Yorty's rope snaked out and got me around the head. It tightened as I hit the end of it, burning every bit of skin from my neck in a swath a half inch to an inch wide. So cruelly was it yanked that it cut off my air and I flopped to the ground, gasping and clawing at the rope with my hands.

Those two, Beechner and Yorty, must have been damned good cowhands once because now Beechner's rope snaked out, catching both of my ankles as easily as a good cowboy would catch both hind feet of a steer.

Now both men backed their horses the same way they would have if they'd been trying to throw a steer. I thought my head was going to be severed from my body and my legs felt like they were being pulled from their sockets. I'd have yelled, but my throat was closed and I couldn't get any breath. Paddock said, "Easy. I don't want the little son-of-a-bitch dead before we find out where the money is."

Both Beechner and Yorty got off their horses. The horses kept the ropes taut enough so I couldn't have got up if I'd tried. I was gagging and choking, and Yorty knelt down and loosened the rope around my neck just enough so that I could get a shallow breath. Then he tied my hands.

Well, I've been mighty hungry in my time, and plenty thirsty on a couple of occasions, and it's sweet to get food when you're starving and water when you're about to die of thirst. But the lack of either water or food can't compare with not getting air when you're close to dying for lack of it.

Paddock said, "All right. Take off his boots. I'll build us a little fire."

So that was what he was going to do. At first anyway. He was going to burn the soles of my feet.

I've always figured I had as much courage as the next man. At least I've always hoped I had. Most men doubt themselves until circumstances prove either that they have the necessary amount of courage or that they don't. After today I'd know. Not that it would do me any good because if I discovered I had the necessary courage it would just get me killed.

My lungs heaved and my belly cramped, trying to get more air. Yorty said, "You'd better loosen that rope some more or we ain't going to get a damn word out of him."

The rope was loosened immediately and I gulped the sweet, life-giving air. I tried to fight but it didn't do me a bit of good. Yorty was tying my feet and Beechner was coiling the ropes they'd used to throw me to the ground. He led the three horses to a nearby clump of scrub cedar trees.

I could smell the fire's smoke. Paddock was squatted beside me looking at me with a gloating grin. "Know what I'm going to do to you, you little bastard?"

Well, I knew he was going to torture me trying to get me to tell where the money was. But I also knew he wasn't going to leave me alive afterward.

His grinning face was only inches from mine. I spit directly into it.

He reared back. Beechner had the bad judgment to laugh. Paddock stood up and aimed a savage kick at my head. I turned my head as he did and the kick landed on my ear.

I felt pain and I tasted brass, and then a curtain of darkness descended over my senses. But before it did, I heard a shot.

I don't know how long I was unconscious. A thin stream of water trickling into my upturned face woke me up. I opened my eyes and turned my head to avoid the stream. Paddock stood over me, pouring water from a canteen into my face. Yorty stood ten or fifteen feet away, gun in hand, looking scared. Beechner was lying where I'd last seen him standing. I remembered his laugh and I remembered the shot and I knew that Beechner's laugh had cost him his life.

Paddock snarled, "All right, let's get started."

Yorty said, "You get started. Jesus, you killed Beechner for nothing more than laughing at you."

Paddock got up and went to the fire. When he came back, he had a smoldering stick of firewood in his hands. He stuck it underneath my nose so that I had to breathe the smoke. I began to cough. Paddock mocked, "Feel the heat, you son-of-a-bitch? You'll feel it more in a minute."

He moved closer to my feet, and I felt the heat of the glowing stick against the soles of my feet. I gritted my teeth and pulled back my feet. He turned his back to me and sat on my legs. He asked, "Where is it? Tell me right now and you'll be none the worse for wear."

I didn't even reply. I knew he was lying. Even if I told

him right now, he wasn't going to spare me either torture or death.

Paddock snarled, "Talk, damn you!" And then I felt the firebrand against the sole of my right foot. I opened my mouth to yell, but Yorty's big dirty hand clamped down on it. I bit his hand and he yanked it away. Then I yelled. I surprised myself because I didn't yell with pain and I didn't beg. I called Paddock every dirty name I'd ever heard, yelling them out at the top of my lungs.

The sole of my right foot was hurting as if the glowing stick was still against it but I knew it wasn't because almost immediately Paddock laid the red hot part of the stick against my foot again, this time starting with the toes and working up, slowly and deliberately like someone would if they were tickling you. I could smell the burning flesh but I kept yelling, kept cussing him. Yorty said, "For God's sake, man . . ." but Paddock only said, "Shut up. I'll make him tell. Give me a hand."

I began struggling even more violently than I had before, and Paddock began cussing me. But Yorty didn't move. He said, "God, I wish I'd never got messed up with you!"

"All right then, I'll do it myself. Maybe it won't be as neat but I'll get it done."

I thought, "Oh, God, I'm done for." I was so damned scared and shocked that I couldn't make a sound. I felt like I was choking, my mouth was so dry. My right foot burned like no pain I'd ever experienced before but I knew it was nothing to the pain that was coming.

Maybe I'd have told him where to find the gold if I'd been able to speak. But I wasn't. All I could do was wait, and watch in horror while he mutilated me.

Suddenly, as shocking in its way as the knife in Paddock's hand, a shot racketed, followed by half a dozen others, in quick succession. Paddock flopped on the ground beside me, dropping the knife and clawing for the revolver that he now kept thrust into his belt. Yorty let out a shout—"Indians!"—and began to run as fast as he could toward the horses. Paddock waited only an instant. Then he pointed the gun at my head and thumbed the hammer back.

I thought he was going to shoot, and I believe he intended to. But then he must have thought about the money and changed his mind. He eased the hammer down, got to his feet and followed Yorty, leaving Beechner dead and me trussed up like a hog.

The three horses that Beechner, Yorty and Paddock had ridden here were now closely bunched in the clump of cedars. They were fidgeting nervously because of the shots and maybe also because of the smell of my burning foot being carried to them on the breeze.

Yorty and Paddock reached them, just as a fresh volley tore into the thicket of cedars. One horse went down, kicking, and continued to kick and thrash around, trying to get up. Paddock and Yorty concealed themselves as best they could and returned the Indians' fire. I lay there helpless in the middle, not knowing when a stray bullet would hit me or when some Apache might kill me just for sport.

I'd given up all hope of surviving when they tied me and Paddock began burning my feet. I still had no hope. But at least I'd die with no more mutilation than the deep burns on my foot.

CHAPTER 17

The burning pain wasn't just in the sole of my foot any longer. It crept up my leg, until there was a savage ache all the way to my hip. I didn't know how the hell I was going to travel even if I did get loose and get away. I couldn't walk on the burned foot, nor could I get a boot on it. The best I'd be able to manage would be a sock. I started to struggle with the ropes that bound me.

An Indian began shooting at me. A bullet tore a furrow two inches from my head, showering me with dirt and filling my eyes with it. Helplessly I lay, trying to blink the dirt out of my eyes, unable to use my hands because they were tied. Tears filled my eyes and I blinked rapidly, trying to increase the flow. The pain in my eyes almost made me forget that in my foot and did temporarily make me forget Paddock, Yorty and the Indians.

I couldn't keep my eyes open and I couldn't keep them closed. I began to curse my predicament with all the anger of which I was capable. But it didn't do any good. I was trussed up like a hog waiting to be slaughtered, my eyes so full of dirt I was practically blind, and I was still being shot at.

Fury made me blink my eyes even more rapidly. Gradually the tears generated by the blinking washed out the dirt and I was able to see again. And now my body tensed, waiting for the impact of that one bullet that would not miss but would strike me in a vital spot and end my life.

There was a flurry of movement nearby and almost instantly Lu was there. She threw herself down beside me, rolling up as close to me as she could. A knife was in her hands and she slashed the ropes that bound my hands, then wriggled down and slashed those that bound my feet. I got no sympathy for my burned feet or streaming eyes from her. She was gone as quickly as she had appeared and, raising my head, I saw her running like a deer straight north toward some boulders in the bottom of the gulch.

Thank God she'd had sense enough to go as soon as she'd cut me loose. If she'd delayed, one of the bullets now being fired so regularly at me might have struck her.

Trying to distract attention from her, I scrambled to where my boots and socks lay and seized them. Then, forcing myself to use and put weight on my burned foot, I limped after her as swiftly as I could.

A bullet struck one of my boots, tore it out of my hand and flung it twenty feet away. My hand stung and I dropped both socks and the other boot. I retrieved them, then hobbled on.

Paddock and Yorty were still holed up in the cedars. They were shooting, but not at me. Instead they were covering me, laying down rapid fire toward the group of rocks where the Indians were. Bullets struck the rocks and whined away.

That was ironic, I thought. Paddock and Yorty were trying to save my life and only minutes before they had been torturing me with the full intention of killing me as soon as they'd got me to tell them where the money was.

I saw Lu dive behind the cover of the boulders toward

which she had been running. She seemed to be unhurt, and I breathed a sigh of relief.

My eyes were still watering from the dirt and I couldn't tell whether some of my tears were because of what Lu had done for me or not. But never in my life before had someone risked their life for mine and the sensation of having someone do so was a little overpowering.

Thinking was, however, something I had no time for then. The pain from my foot was so terrible as I stepped on a rock that I sprawled headlong. But I was getting madder all the time. On hands and knees I crawled toward the boulders where Lu had concealed herself. Paddock and Yorty were still shooting at the Indians. Lu, with a Spencer she had kept with her, was shooting at Paddock and Yorty. Only all this covering fire made it possible to reach the boulders and rejoin Lu.

The first thing I said was, "Are you all right?"

She nodded. My head was spinning and I didn't know what to do next. She had a Spencer, but I didn't know how much ammunition she had for it. We were part of a triangle, Indians on one corner, Paddock and Yorty on another, and us on the third.

I sat down to put on my two socks and grabbed the remaining boot, which I hoped was for the uninjured foot. It was. Carefully, gingerly, I put a sock on my right foot. I put sock and boot on the other one. Now, by walking on my toes with my right foot, and putting full weight on my left, I'd be able to travel slowly, even if painfully.

I asked, "How much ammunition have you got for that gun?"

She fumbled in a pouch tied to the leather thong that held her legging up and brought out about a dozen cartridges. I asked, "How many left in the gun?"

She didn't know. I began reloading. The gun took five before it was full, which meant I now had fourteen in the gun, seven in my hand.

I could see the two horses belonging to Paddock and Yorty even if I could not see the men. I laid down, rested the gun barrel on a rock, and took careful aim on the chest of the closest one. I squeezed the trigger with as much care as I ever had. The gun roared and smoke puffed out before me. When it cleared enough to see, the horse was down.

Quickly now, I took aim on the second horse. Both Paddock and Yorty were now trying to reach him and the Indians across the clearing all let go at once with their single-shot trapdoor rifles. I fired and the second horse went down.

Now, infuriated because I had put them afoot, both Paddock and Yorty turned their attention from the Indians to us. Bullets ricocheted off the rocks behind which we were hidden and whined away into space.

As much as I was hurting, I couldn't suppress a grin. Lu asked, "What do we do now?"

"Wait until they've emptied their guns. Then maybe we can slip away."

"I've got horses. But they're half a mile away. You can't make it that far."

"I can make it clear of Paddock and Yorty and those Indians. Then you can bring the horses."

The firing from Paddock and Yorty had stopped. That from the Indians was spasmodic and their bullets weren't fired at us but at Paddock and Yorty directly across from them.

I should have killed both Paddock and Yorty after I'd killed their horses, I thought. They'd been exposed for several minutes while they were trying to reach the remaining unhurt horse. I could have killed both of them just as easily as I killed that remaining horse.

But I hadn't even thought of it and now I admitted to myself that I couldn't have done it anyway. I wanted Lu but if I was her husband's killer that would stand between us as long as we lived. At least it would as far as I was concerned.

There was an exposed place about fifty feet from the pile of boulders, and when she came to it, Lu crossed it by pressing herself closer to the ground. I crawled to where I could see the cedars where Paddock and Yorty were. I fired four shots into them, and as the first one roared, Lu got up and ran like a deer until she reached a bend in the gully that afterward protected her.

She stopped and waited there for me, but I waved her on. Reluctantly and with a lingering backward glance, she disappeared.

She'd be back with the horses in fifteen or twenty minutes, I thought. By the time she did get back, I had to be across that exposed place and around the bend, hidden from both Yorty and Paddock and the Indians, but able to discourage any pursuit with the remaining cartridges in the Spencer carbine.

For some strange reason Paddock and Yorty once again shifted targets and began firing an almost steady barrage at the Indians' hiding place. Bullets struck the rocks and whined away. I began swiftly to scramble up across the open place toward the bend where Lu had earlier disappeared.

I got halfway across it before I was seen. Even as Paddock and Yorty began firing, I realized that the boulders hid me from the rocks where the Indians were.

And neither Paddock nor Yorty dared shoot to kill. They had to be careful, shooting only to cripple me so that they could torture the location of the money out of me before I died.

Bullets struck behind me and twice right beside my legs, but nothing struck my flesh. I reached the bend, crawled behind it, then turned and laid a couple of shots into the cedars, forcing Paddock and Yorty to yank their heads down at once.

What had been an impossible situation, a hopeless one, had suddenly been turned around, due firstly to the intervention of the small band of Apaches, but due also to Lu's incredible courage in running across that open ground to cut me loose.

Occasionally I peeked around the rock behind which I lay prone, checking to see if either Paddock or Yorty had succeeded in getting away. They had not. The Indian gunfire and the barren hillside behind them kept them in place.

Now, I thought, all I had to do was wait. Lu had horses and had gone after them. She'd be returning with them soon, and since she knew the positions of both Apaches and the two white men, she would be able to choose a route coming back that would be safe.

At least that was what I thought. A single gunshot changed my mind. It was ahead and sounded as if it could not be more than a couple of hundred yards away.

I got up. It was then I realized that my revolver was missing from its holster. I remembered Paddock taking it, but I didn't remember what he had done with it. It was possible, but damned unlikely, that Lu had it and that she had used it against an Indian or Indians trying to halt her progress with the horses.

Now was no time for me to favor my badly burned foot. Lu had unhesitatingly exposed herself to cut me loose. It was my turn to get her out of whatever predicament she was in.

I ran, nearly falling every time I stepped on a rock because no matter how determined I was and how strong my will, the pain in my foot made the leg muscles weak, sometimes nearly made them give out.

This was an area of scrub cedars and high rabbit brush, among which was a ground cover of grass and prickly-pear cactus. If I stepped on one of those I'd go down for sure.

I heard an Apache call to another in the Apache tongue, which I didn't understand. Wanting to draw them toward me instead of toward Lu, I yelled, "Lu! Here I am!"

I drew them to me all right. I saw them suddenly through the trees, less than thirty yards away. I halted, raised the Spencer and downed one of them with my first shot. They were only boys, and immediately the other one dropped to the ground beside the first.

I knew how little time we had. If Lu didn't reach me with the horses in the next couple of minutes, we'd have both Paddock and Yorty *and* the band of Apaches coming after us.

Listening, I heard the sound of a horse off to my left, away from the young Apache I'd shot and his friend, who had flopped down beside him. I turned and, trying to watch both the ground and the land around me, I made my way as swiftly as I could toward the sounds I'd heard.

I didn't have to go very far. I saw the two horses and I saw Lu, being careful to keep herself all but hidden behind one of them. They were Indian ponies, with rope hackamores and blankets on their backs in lieu of saddles.

I reached her. I was scared when I saw fresh red blood seeping through the bandage on her arm, running down it in rivulets. I said, "Oh, my God! You've hurt your arm again."

She shook her head impatiently. "Get mounted. We haven't time to talk about that."

She was right, of course, because the wound certainly hadn't incapacitated her. I leaped astride the short Apache pony and followed her as she wound her way through the grove of cedars at a walk. Only when we reached open ground did she drum on the horse's sides with her heels and urge him to a gallop. She cut to the right and after a few minutes we reached the broad trail left by the two troops of cavalry.

Still galloping recklessly, she turned into it. Once she looked back. I could tell that the blood had stopped flowing from the wound in her upper shoulder because now all I could see was drying blood. She shouted, "Did you tell them?"

If I'd been an Apache, she wouldn't have even asked. She'd have known. But I was white. And I was young. I shook my head.

She nodded with a little smile and turned her head back toward the front. The nod and the smile told me she had never really believed that I'd told them where the money was. She'd just had to ask.

I still wanted Paddock nearly as bad as I wanted the money. But I had a feeling I wouldn't have to go looking for him. He'd come after me. What I had to do was make damn sure he never caught me with my defenses down the way he had last time.

CHAPTER 18

For a good hour we galloped along in the wake of Captain Dennison's two troops. I rode in the lead, and Lu rode about fifteen or twenty feet behind. Several times I looked back, searching her face with my eyes.

I wanted Lu more than ever. Maybe I was only eighteen, but I was man enough to know that much. Every time I looked back, I searched her eyes and face for some expression that would let me know she felt the same.

Apaches are supposed to be inscrutable, and I suppose to the average man's eyes, Lu's expression would have been inscrutable. But not to me. The glow in her eyes was soft, the slight curve of her lips the same. She was mine. She would go with me.

A lone trooper came galloping back along the trail, drew up before me and fell in beside me. I noticed that he did not salute and that there was no deference in his voice. He said, "Sonny, the captain wants to see you. On the double."

That word "Sonny" made my face flush with anger. Damn Dennison anyway. Where the hell did he get off calling me "Sonny" when it was me who had alerted the fort? When it was me who had captured Paddock and discovered the evidence of his crimes? When it was me who had recovered not only the money stolen from Satterfield's store, but that Paddock had stolen from his many victims?

Besides that, the damned trooper wasn't much older than I was. I said, "Sonny, you go back and tell your captain that I'll be along when it damn pleases me."

I was being childish and knew it, but I had got to the point where I didn't care. I was tired of being treated like a kid. Marshal McCabe wouldn't do it after he knew the things that I had done. And I didn't see why I had to put up with it from strangers.

Lu rode up beside me. Her eyes told me she understood, but she asked anyway, "Why did you do that?"

I was hot under the collar still. I said, "I'm getting goddamn tired of being treated like a kid."

"Are you going to report to him?"

I thought about that. If I did, he'd probably just give me hell for falling behind even though I was a civilian and not subject in any way to his authority. Lu and I might accompany the two troops to the stagecoach way station, but our usefulness in driving off the Apaches would be nil.

A new idea was forming in my mind. The trouble between Captain Dennison's two troops and the Apaches might be offering me a never-to-be-repeated opportunity. While the Army, the people at the way station and the Apaches were occupied, I might very well be able to recover the gunnysacks of money and make it back to Alkali Flat. Certainly it would be the last thing Paddock and Yorty would expect of me. And they were afoot. They knew my foot was so sore I couldn't walk on it, and could hardly ride. They'd expect me to join the two troops of cavalry, get my foot treated by the surgeon and then, probably, ride in the ambulance.

Lu was watching me, a puzzled look on her face. "What *are* you going to do?" I thought that at least *she* didn't treat me like a kid. She looked to me to make whatever decisions were to be made, and once I had made them, she accepted them without question.

I said, "If Paddock and Yorty get horses they're going to be coming soon. If we stay with the cavalry, they'll get another crack at us. Dennison isn't going to let me ride with this foot, so you can bet we'll be separated unless you ride in the ambulance with me."

"I can do that."

"Maybe he won't let you." All this time I'd been keeping my eyes on the road. Marshal McCabe had not only taught me to track but he'd also taught me how to hide a track. Rocky draws kept feeding into the road at regular intervals and as soon as the trooper was completely out of sight, I said, "Come on. Stay on the rocks as much as you can."

I turned into a rocky draw and Lu followed me. We were riding barefooted horses, so their hoofs left little mark. I couldn't ride with my foot in the stirrup, unless I could balance my weight on my rump and hold on to the horse's mane.

The troopers were gone and the messenger had no way of knowing we'd left the road, so it would probably be a long time before Dennison realized we were gone. We climbed steeply to the top of a ridge where there was a clump of cedars. I slid off my horse and gave the reins to Lu. I accidentally hit my foot against a rock, and cursed angrily.

We'd ridden considerably past the turnoff that led to the Indian agency but I wasn't about to risk running into a bunch of Apaches by going back to the road. So we stayed in the cedars and rocks.

I held my horse to a steady trot and Lu kept pace behind. Before long we spotted the agency buildings and the stable. The new stableman was working in the corral out back. I made a sign for Lu to stay with the two horses, then I started painfully down the hillside on foot, careful to keep the stable between me and the stableman. We needed fresh horses. But we couldn't steal them and if we let the stableman know of our presence, he'd pass on the fact that we'd been here to Paddock and Yorty when they arrived and furthermore he'd tell them exactly which direction we'd gone so they wouldn't have to waste a lot of time picking up our trail.

I reached the stable and turned my head to look at Lu. She was standing still, almost invisible beside the thick, twisted trunk of a cedar tree.

The floor was covered with dry manure so I didn't make any noise hobbling along through it. I saw a pitchfork and changed course enough to pick it up. It would work pretty well as a crutch.

I started up the ladder. I couldn't put any weight on my burned foot but I had the pitchfork and my hands so I got along pretty well.

I reached the top finally, and with a scoop I took most of the grain out of the full barrel and put it into the other one. As soon as I could see the gunnysacks, I got hold of one corner and pulled. Oats rained down from them, making what seemed like a lot of noise, but I figured the stableman would be making plenty of noise of his own down in the corral and likely wouldn't hear it. I slung them over my shoulder, limped painfully back to the ladder and then climbed down. When I reached the door, Lu was still in the same position, absolutely motionless, so I took a good look around and then headed straight toward her, still using the fork for a crutch. I reached Lu, slung the gunnysacks over my horse's withers and vaulted to his back. Immediately afterward, I got two revolvers out of the sack and gave one to Lu.

There was a temptation to gallop away, but I resisted it. Carefully keeping the stable between us and the stableman, I held the horses to a walk until we had gone over a hill and were lost to sight. Even then, I didn't kick my horse's ribs because I knew he'd still make a lot of noise crashing through the brush.

Finally I stopped, in sight of the road. Lu asked, "What are you going to do now? Your foot is hurting terrible. It ought to be treated by the surgeon and you ought to get off of it."

"Paddock and Yorty are probably with the captain's troops by now."

"They won't be for very long. When they find out you and I have gone . . . We *could* go back and rejoin the captain's troops."

I thought about that. The plan had appeal and my foot *was* killing me. On the other hand, it wasn't going to take Paddock and Yorty long to trail us to the agency and back again. And even if Paddock wasn't able to get to me in the ambulance he'd be able to get to Lu easily enough.

"You'd have to ride in the ambulance with me. I don't want to give Paddock any chance to get to you."

"I can do that."

I nodded. "Sure you can if the captain will let you. And then both of us will be sitting ducks for Paddock and Yorty. They know by now that they're not going to get me to tell them where the money is. But they also know that the minute they put an iron on you, I'll tell them anything they want to know."

Despite what she had endured, I had never seen tears in her eyes. But I saw them now. "You'd do that? For me?"

"Of course I would."

"Maybe the captain would put a guard over us."

"I doubt it. Even if he did, Paddock and Yorty could overcome the guard."

"Then what *are* you going to do?"

"I've been thinking. Dennison is heading for that way station as fast as he can travel. When he gets there, he's going to have a battle on his hands. Paddock and Yorty will join him until they find out we're not with him. Then they'll back-track, and they'll either find our trail or guess where the money is. I figure on taking the shortest route to Alkali Flat. Paddock and Yorty can't get this money away from a whole damn town. Not if they're on guard."

"And after that?"

I could feel my face flushing, but I spoke determinedly. "Well, you and I both know that no Arizona town is going to let you live there and treat you the way you deserve to be treated. So we'll go away. We can go east to New Mexico, or Colorado, or to any of a dozen other places."

Tears were now running unashamedly across her dusky cheeks. For lack of something else to say, I said, "I never saw an Apache cry."

"We're no different than anybody else. Maybe we don't cry as easily but we cry."

We were wasting time, sitting here talking. There was no telling where Paddock and Yorty were. We descended to the road as rapidly as we could, and crossed it where a dry gully had carried flash floods across it for centuries. We rode up the steep gulch for a quarter mile. By then both our horses were sweating and breathing hard. I said, "Let's get off and rest them. We can see the road and we can see whether Paddock and Yorty pick up the place we crossed the road."

She didn't reply, but I was getting used to her now. If she didn't answer me it meant she agreed.

I handed her my horse's reins and she led both animals back and well out of sight. I hunkered down to wait behind a rock, where I could hardly be seen.

I knew this was gambling. If Paddock and Yorty came along the road and *did* pick up our trail, we were in trouble because we'd be less than a mile ahead of them.

On the other hand, if they passed the spot where we'd crossed we'd be in the clear.

What I was betting on was that Paddock and Yorty would have obtained horses, reached Dennison and talked to the trooper. They'd have gotten, from him, the place he'd seen us last. If that was so, they'd pass this place at a hard gallop and wouldn't see anything.

Sure enough, in the distance, I heard the pound of hoofs. Lu came up at my side with complete silence. Holding our breath, we waited.

Neither Paddock nor Yorty even slowed. They passed the spot where we had crossed the road at a hard lope. The sound of their horses' hoofbeats died, and we were all alone.

CHAPTER 19

The hoofbeats died, but that didn't mean all sound died. A flurry of rifle shots barked, their sounds unmistakable. They were the reports of the old single-shot, .50 caliber trapdoor rifles that most of the Apaches used. They had ridden into an ambush.

The volley was followed by the sharper bark of handguns, and by one shot, which I recognized as that of a Spencer carbine. It made a sound louder than that of the handguns, sharper than those of the Indians' guns. Then there was silence.

I had already mounted. Now I hauled my horse to a halt. Lu looked questioningly at me. She said, "You want them dead. You hate them. They are dangerous to you. Why, then, do you stop?"

They had tortured me. They would have done much worse if they'd had the time and opportunity. They wanted the money I carried in the gunnysacks slung across the horse's withers in front of me. And what Lu said made sense. If they could they'd get the money and then kill me. They'd take Lu with them and she'd be just as much Yorty's property as she would Paddock's. Marriage vows meant nothing to him, nor did Lu herself.

But there *was* something. I tried to tell myself that I wanted to capture Paddock and bring him to justice for the mass murders he had committed. But deep down I knew it wasn't that. No matter what Paddock had done, I couldn't let him die the way the Apaches would make him die.

I took the gunnysacks from in front of me and handed them to Lu. "These go to Alkali Flat in case I don't make it back. There ought to be a reward for them."

She asked, "What are you going to do? Surely you're not going to risk your life for *them!*"

"No. I'm not going to try and rescue them. But I know how the Apaches will make them die. I can't let that happen."

She looked at me as if I was out of my mind, but there was something else in the way she looked at me. It made me feel good. She said, "I will wait."

"No!" I said emphatically. "As soon as I leave, you must leave too. Travel as fast as you can. If they catch you, you know what they'll do to you."

She looked rebellious. I said, "I have never asked anything of you, but I am asking now. Will you do it?"

She met my glance for several moments. Tears dimmed her eyes but at last she nodded. "I will do as you ask."

Now, with that off my mind, I whirled my horse and pounded toward the sound of the shots as rapidly as I could. Either Paddock and Yorty had escaped or they were already prisoners. I knew that the Apaches, wanting to take them prisoners, would have shot their horses, rather than trying to shoot them. They didn't want the horses; they wanted the men.

I rode at a hard gallop for what I judged to be a quarter mile. Then I drew my horse back to a walk. Not long afterward, I spotted a group of horses, two of them dead, and a dozen or so Indians clustered around two white men on the ground.

They had already stripped the men naked. I could see a bloody wound on Yorty, but Paddock seemed to have no wounds other than his broken arm. He was struggling, but struggling did him no good. In minutes, they had secured his hands and feet with rawhide thongs. Yorty lay silent, appearing to be dead. The Indians didn't even bother tying him.

One of the Indians knelt over Paddock's body as soon as it was secured. He had a knife in his hand.

I knew I was a fool. Paddock wouldn't do this for me. If I did what I intended to do, I'd have every one of these Indians on my trail immediately.

And all I had now was the Navy Colt's I had dug out of the gunnysack. The range for it was much too great. I crept down the slope, trying to stay hidden, knowing that if I didn't hurry I'd be too late for what I meant to do.

The Indian laughed in Paddock's face, and said something to him that sounded like a taunt. Paddock began to struggle even more violently.

I'd never have made it had not the Indians' interest been centered on Paddock. I finished traveling the last hundred yards at the best kind of run I could manage, careless of the noise I might be making. The Indians' horses were making enough noise fidgeting around to cover any noise that I might make and I couldn't be quiet because of my foot.

Finally I stopped. I raised the revolver and, holding it firmly in both hands, sighted carefully on Paddock's chest. Furiously I cursed the unsteadiness of my hands, but it was fire now or give it up. At any time one of the Indians would turn his head and see me and then it would be too late.

The sights steadied and I squeezed the trigger. I knew

the instant I fired that I had scored a hit. Paddock's body jerked from the bullet's impact and then lay still.

The Indians instantly turned to me. I still had four loads in the .36 caliber Colt's. As rapidly as I could, I shot four of the Indians' horses. I saw each one fall.

Then the Indians were running toward me, shooting as they came. I whirled and limped up the hillside, knowing I had been a fool. I had saved Paddock mutilation but in the end what difference did it make? He would have died anyway.

I'd told Lu to head for Alkali Flat but thank God she hadn't obeyed. Suddenly I saw her coming, riding her own horse recklessly, trailing mine behind.

She reached me. I yelled, "Your gun! Give me your gun!"

She did, and I handed her mine in exchange and after that some cartridges from my belt. She immediately began reloading it.

I snatched the reins of my horse. "Now go, damn it! Go!"

She didn't hesitate this time. She spurred up the hillside. I raised the gun she had given me, and just as I had before, held it in both hands and carefully sighted, not at men but at horses. They made bigger targets, were easier to hit, and would, for each one I hit, keep an Apache from following.

Five shots. I hit only three horses this time while bullets cut twigs and ricocheted off rocks close to me. As soon as the gun was empty I vaulted to the horse's back and thundered away after Lu.

My horse flinched and I knew he had been grazed in the leg. He might have stopped but I wouldn't let him. I held the reins up and used my left foot to kick him with.

The horse limped along in much the way I had been limping earlier.

I couldn't let him stop. Upon his continuing depended my life and maybe Lu's as well, because if she thought I was in trouble, she'd come back to help.

The wound must have been a flesh wound because the horse's leg, the right rear one, did not give way. He limped, and slowed, but the belaboring of my pistol barrel on his rump kept him lunging awkwardly up the hill.

Quite possibly, the wound threw his gait off enough to make the Indians miss. In any case, I reached the crest of the ridge to find Lu waiting for me.

I yelled, "I could use another horse. Is your gun reloaded?"

She nodded, proffering the gun. I gave her my own and some cartridges for it, took hers, then cut her horse across the rump with the barrel of the gun. The animal jumped, but he took off down the slope. She did not seem to be trying to hold him in. I knew she'd have been willing to stand beside me in the coming fight. But she realized she might be more useful if she could intervene later.

I tied my horse. Then I found a rock and squatted behind it. Four Apaches, riding hard, came into sight. I rested the gun on the rock and carefully aimed at the chest of the first oncoming horse, completely ignoring the man riding him. I fired, the horse went down and the Indian was thrown nearly ten feet beyond.

Instantly the other three separated, veering to right and left. I got a bead on a second one and he also went down. I got a third before the last one got out of range.

It was doubtful if any of the Indians would try pursuing us because they only had one horse left. I untied my horse, mounted, and rode up the hill after Lu. In minutes I reached the crest, saw her ahead of me, and then headed down the steep hill toward her. For an instant back there I'd almost completely forgotten my foot. At least I'd been able to function in spite of it.

Now it hurt like hell. I'd put weight on it, I'd scraped it and I'd torn flesh from it. My sock, what was left of it, was a mass of fresh blood.

We were all the way to the bottom of the hill and I was crossing a small clearing of light-colored sand when the shot racketed from the crest of the hill behind me. My horse went down, throwing me against the base of a heavy clump of brush. Lu didn't make a sound, but in an instant she was off her horse and beside me.

Lu and her horse were both hidden behind the brush clump and there wasn't time to urge her to flee. I said softly, "Stay behind your horse."

I moved out away from the brush. It was a moment before I could see the oncoming Apache but I could sure as hell hear him. He was coming at a reckless, hard gallop and I thought he'd run me down before I even got a look at him. I finally saw him, though, about twenty feet away. He was coming so fast and the horse was zigzagging back and forth so much that I couldn't get a clear shot to save my life. And I didn't want to hurt the horse.

In an instant he'd seen Lu and her horse behind the huge clump of brush so I couldn't wait for him to come to me. I had to go to him. Through some kind of miracle I was able to force myself to forget my foot and run straight up the slope toward him.

His horse saw me and shied and I leaped up, grabbed the Indian's breechclout with one hand, rammed the revolver against his body with the other and fired.

The horse's momentum carried him on past, throwing both me and the Indian aside. Lu leaped out from behind the cactus and seized the horse's halter rope.

I was looking for the Indian because I didn't know whether he was dead or not. Limping now, I made my way in the direction he had been thrown and in a few seconds I encountered his body. There was no breathing. He was dead.

I stuck the gun into my holster, took the rope from Lu and vaulted to the horse's back. I caught up with Lu almost immediately, glancing quickly at her horse's withers to make sure the gunnysacks were there.

And now nothing stood between Lu and me. Paddock was dead. We would have our own house, maybe kids . . .

Lu turned her head, smiling at me. Her glance went beyond, looking for danger. She didn't see any, and I doubted if we'd see any more Apaches between here and Alkali Flat.

But I had trouble facing me up ahead sure enough. I had to face Marshal McCabe, who was counting on me to take over the deputy marshal's job as soon as I was twenty-one.

I had to face Sue Ann Satterfield, even if I wasn't committed to her and even if I knew damned well I wasn't the kind of man she wanted anyhow.

Most serious of all, I had to plan, with Lu, some kind of life for both of us. And I hadn't the slightest idea what it was going to be. I only knew one thing for sure. I wasn't ever going to give her up.

The only way I'd let Lu go back to San Carlos was if she was hungry and in rags. And I figured I was man enough to see it never came to that.

CHAPTER 20

We traveled for several hours, holding the horses to a walk and trying to travel as quietly as possible.

Finally we topped the last rise and could look out across the wide plain. In the far distance I could hear the mournful wail of the train.

Unexpectedly Lu asked, "I've been thinking and there's something I want to know. Why did you do that?"

"Do what?"

"Go back and risk your life to save him pain?"

"Paddock?" I had thought about that myself. The truth was, I didn't know why I'd done it. What I did know was that he wouldn't have done it for me if our positions had been reversed, but then I liked to think I was a better man than Paddock was.

I grinned at Lu in the darkness. "Probably because white men are plain damn fools. I knew I couldn't save his life but I didn't want him to die in the kind of pain they had planned for him." I thought a minute and then I added, "Or maybe I just wanted to be sure he was really dead."

She turned her head back to the front without comment. I said, "We'll be getting back to Alkali Flat pretty soon. And you haven't got a husband anymore."

She didn't turn her head. I said, "You belong to me now."

Without looking around she said, "You can't get a job as long as I am with you."

"Jobs are a dime a dozen. Women like you come along maybe once in a lifetime."

"What about the white girl in town?"

"She didn't want me before and she won't want me now. And I don't want her. Not after knowing you."

We rode out until we reached the railroad tracks. We sat down on a tie, close together against the early morning chill. Lu asked, "Why are we waiting here?"

"I figure we can ride into town in style."

Lu was shivering and I knew it wasn't altogether from the cold. She said, "Jason Cole, you are a fool. Why don't you marry your white girl in Alkali Flat. You can run her store for her."

I said, "Hell, she wouldn't marry me. She always was lukewarm about me. She's been coddled and pampered all her life and she'll want a man who'll go on doing it, which I won't.

"Besides that, the only time she ever showed any interest in me was when I took out after her pa's killer when nobody else would. And anyhow she's a useless kind of woman and after seeing the way a real woman behaves when the chips are down, nobody like her could ever satisfy me."

"I am an Apache."

I said, "By God, will you quit apologizing for being an Apache? I doubt if there's any race of people in history that's put up a better fight against ten or twenty times their number. It's time you started feeling proud."

She didn't say anything more but she moved closer to me and she put her hand on my arm. She snuggled up closer and pretty soon she stopped shivering. I heard the train whistle, no more'n a quarter mile away this time.

She asked, "How do you know they'll stop for you?"

I toed the gunnysacks we'd hauled so long, so far. "When they see who it is and they see these, they'll stop for us. Let's build a little fire so they can tell who it is."

"All right." Her tone was pleased. She had never ridden on a train.

I built a small grass fire and added some dead cholla sticks to it. By the time the train arrived, it was burning brightly enough so they could see us pretty good. I waved my hands and the train pulled to a squealing halt.

The door of one of the coaches opened and I could see why they hadn't been afraid of us. A couple of dozen rifles pointed at us from the open windows of the two coaches nearest us. I said, "We're headin' into Alkali Flat. I'm a deputy marshal there. How about a ride?"

Someone yelled, "Deputy hell! It's that kid that works for McCabe!"

"Who you got with you?"

"An Apache girl."

"What you goin' to do with them horses? We can't—"

"We'll turn 'em loose. They're Apache ponies and they'll eventually go home."

"All right. Come on aboard." The conductor had a lantern now and he looked us over carefully as we climbed up the steps with me limping pretty bad and Lu helping me. I took Lu's hand and led her into one of the coaches. We found a couple of empty seats and she slid in by the window so she could watch the countryside go by. I heard a man yell, "Looks like it was all right. There was only the two of them."

I had the gunnysacks but nobody knew what was in

them. I wasn't going to tell, either. I laid them down at my feet. I knew we were safe at last, but it still rankled to be called a kid.

When we reached town it turned out that Marshal McCabe was on the platform in Alkali Flat. He hadn't had any more success getting up a posse than I had. I said, "I got all the money from Mr. Satterfield's safe."

He was big and some on the heavy side. He put a hand on my shoulder that felt like it weighed fifty pounds, and then he asked, "Who's this?"

"It's a long story, Mr. McCabe. But treat her right; I'm going to marry her. Whether you keep me on and give me a deputy's job when I'm twenty-one I guess depends on what you think of Apache girls. But one way or another, I'm going to marry her. She's a lot of woman, Mr. McCabe. More'n I'm ever likely to meet up with again."

He took the gunnysacks. "There's more here than was taken from Satterfield."

"Yes, sir. Her husband, Nathan Paddock, made a business of robbing travelers."

"And Paddock?"

"He's dead."

"Well," he said, "you two are tired. You want to marry this girl before I put you up in a room at the hotel?"

That was a sign of respect for Lu that I was grateful for. I said, "It's early in the morning. Can you get the preacher out?"

"I'll get him out."

We headed up the street, while the train hissed and finally puffed out of the station behind us.

Marshal McCabe said, "Come on, you two. Can't have you sharin' a hotel room unless you're married, can we?"

Right then I thought I didn't need to worry about a job with the United States marshal's office. One way or another, Marshal McCabe would manage it. And if I knew Marshal McCabe, the people in Alkali Flat would, by God, accept Lu like she was one of their own.

I began to think of being alone with Lu. And I'm afraid that was all I thought about throughout the marriage ceremony and everything that followed it. It seemed like forever, but at last the door of the hotel room closed behind us. And, smiling, she came into my arms.

A0003200042384